AND IF / THAT

mockingbird

DON'T / SING

AND IF / THAT mockingbird DON'T / SING

PARENTING STORIES GONE SPECULATIVE

75 FLASH BY 76 AUTHORS

EDITED BY HANNAH GRIECO

Alternating Current Press
Boulder, Colorado

Alternating Current
Boulder, Colorado
alternatingcurrentarts.com

ISBN: 978-1-946580-32-0
First Edition: January 2022

FOR AVI, KAI, AND MILA

To describe my mother would be to write
about a hurricane in its perfect power.
Or the climbing, falling colors of a rainbow.
　　　　　　　—Maya Angelou

"I was scared," she said, and then uttered a shaky little laugh.
"I guess you don't know what scared is
until one of your kids screams in the dark."
　　　　　—Stephen King, *Christine*

LETTER FROM THE *editor*

W hen I began writing, all I wrote were parenting essays. Essays in a thousand words or so, with a neat little beginning, middle, and end. There was always a problem to be solved, always a clear path forward, and everything got resolved around eight hundred words in, with a paragraph or two of reflection afterward. A neat little present tied with a neat little bow. The end.

These essays did well. They landed in good publications and made my own parents proud. But sometimes, every once in a while, I'd slip in something horrible and real. Something that lurked under the surface. I'd write a sentence, somewhere hidden in the middle, about how I wasn't so sure about motherhood. About whether I was able to keep doing it, or about whether or not I *wanted* to keep doing it. About moments of anger so big I thought they might swallow me, or moments where I felt like I was sinking, shrinking, crumbling.

About being nothing more than "mother," and failing even at that. About needing, desperately, to be more.

The messages I received after publishing these pieces were dramatic. Grandmothers felt sorry for my children, strangers threatened acts of violence, and some shocked mothers called me abusive or neglectful. But email after email from other mothers whispered: *yes, yes, yes.*

So, I started writing more sentences that told the truth. I left the problems unsolved, or solved them messily, humanly, and imperfectly. I redefined love and motherhood in my head and in my writing, abandoning sainthood and the impossible, chafing expectations that saturated my daily life. I wrote hard words. I wrote fewer essays for established parenting magazines and instead wrote shorter, more vulnerable literary works. Sometimes true, sometimes fiction—but fiction is still true on some level, isn't it? If there's a vampire, there is a lust for blood underneath her story. If there's a ghost, there's a fear of, or fascination with, death.

I wanted to read more stories about what parenting really felt like to others. Not the Hallmark-card variety, but the 3 a.m.-insomnia parenting. The fear parenting. The anger, the grief, the love-bigger-than-all-of-it parenting—beautiful not because of its perfection, but because of its ugly persistence. Its messy, human, imperfect beauty.

When I put out the call for submissions to this flash anthology, the response was enormous. Writers from all over the world sent in their speculative parenting stories. And we redefined *speculative*, too. Supernatural, horror, fantasy—but also the stories nobody wants or expects parents to tell. Speculative because these stories aren't supposed to exist. But they do. They breathe, they rage, they laugh, they scream, and they fly.

Thank you for reading this book, and thank you for giving space to what's real and scary and strange in the act of parenting our children.

Hannah Grieco
December 20, 2021

TABLE OF *contents*

PART ONE: *shadows*

PART TWO: *teeth*

PART THREE: *cages*

MATTER: *miscellany*

AND IF / THAT *mockingbird* DON'T / SING

PART / ONE :
shadows

LISTEN

Leslie Walker Trahan

I don't like telling stories, but tonight I make an exception. A storm is coming, and my daughter is already in bed with a blanket pulled up to her chin. "There once was a girl," I say, "an orphan." I give the girl a foe to fight, a curse to lift. Something, a bird perhaps, beats against the window. "What is that?" my daughter asks. "Don't worry," I say. The girl in the story gets a few wins—a truth uncovered, a power revealed. But a good story is not always easy to tell. There are losses, too. Her loyal confidant, her home, her village. "Who is knocking at the window?" my daughter asks. "No one," I say, "it's just the rain." In the story, I introduce a new villain, one more dangerous than any the girl has known before. The girl is frightened where she thought she would be fearless, ambivalent where she thought she would be unwavering. Her powers, so recently revealed, fail her at a critical moment. The girl wonders things she's never wondered before. How did this conflict start? What really happened to her parents? Why is there no one to protect her? She is a child, after all. And what is she to make of those strange dreams she's been having? Bared teeth, blood stains on her hands. My daughter looks up, eyes wide: "What happens now?" When the villain arrives, the girl turns away. She once thought the fight was the purpose of her life, but she no longer believes the purpose of a life can be so thinly cataloged. She puts down her weapons, and the villain, seeing the girl's hesitation, falters. Outside, the rain's battering is fierce but rhythmic. My daughter rests her head against her pillow. "This story is too long," she says—"Get to the battle already." "There is no battle," I say, "only a girl." My daughter yawns. Her eyes become slits. "I get it," she says. "No, you don't," I tell her. *"Listen."* I pinch her legs. I pinch her arms. I pinch her cheeks, the ones I used to kiss as she was falling asleep. "Listen," I whisper into her already-dreaming ears. *"There is more."*

BAD BOYS

Aubrey Hirsch

They seemed like accidents at first: Jacob's heel in the soft tissue of her diaphragm, Harley's head bouncing off her cheekbone. Perhaps I was tickling them too hard, Stella mused as she cataloged her new bruises after putting the boys to bed.

What parent didn't have an inventory of accidental injuries inflicted by their offspring? Stella sometimes talked about them with the other moms and dads at the park: a black eye from a pitched ball too swiftly returned, a rolled ankle from a clumsy bump on the stairs, a pinched finger from a falling toybox lid. After each story, the parents would laugh together in a reassuring way. Isn't it funny, what these children do to us?

But the further the boys got from toddlerhood, the more calculated these mishaps seemed to be. Like Harley waiting for the exact moment her index finger landed on the jamb to slam the door. Or when Jacob abruptly dismounted from her shoulders, a limp lock of her hair still clutched in each hand.

"Ouch," she would say gently, pointing to the blooming flush, or beading blood, or gathering film of pus, "that hurts Mama." The boys would offer bashful smiles she once interpreted as apologetic, but now read as faintly joyful. "Ouch," she'd say again, letting the pain creep into her voice a little. "That hurts."

Stella asked her husband, "Are they hurting you?"

"Hm?"

"The boys. Are they hurting you?"

"Hurting me? No."

"They're hurting me," she said.

"You're smaller than I am," he said. "Maybe I just don't notice it." His work was waiting. Stella could always tell when he was done with a conversation.

She'd stopped telling the stories at the park, as well. The reassuring laughter had long since faded to worried glances. The other parents' expressions were no longer amused but sympathetic. They seemed to be avoiding her. Sometimes she caught Harley's eye from across the playground. He wasn't looking at her, not really. He was looking at her parts.

The boys hunted in the yard for spiders and worms to bring into her bed. Jacob found an injured bee with its stinger still intact and hid it in the sleeve of her sweater. There was something primal about their behavior, instinctual even. Before they learned to tie their shoes, the boys could loop the long silhouettes of their footie pajamas into nooses. When she took away their craft scissors, they chewed their nails to points, sharpened their teeth on the chipped ceramic edges of the bathtub.

The more she thought about it, the further back it went. Jacob's shallow latch, pulling her nipples like taffy. The way Harley picked at her skin when she rocked him. How they seemed to divide up the night, each hungry in a different hour, so that she could never really rest.

Further back than that, even: the morning sickness, the excessive weight gain—even for twins, the way they shifted around each other in her womb to rub their bones over her most vulnerable parts. For weeks they took turns kicking her ribs, one firing up just as the other drifted off to sleep. The obstetrician who inspected her busted bones said he'd never seen such symmetrical fractures.

And now they came at her with brightly painted blocks, with heavy-booted action figures, with splinters peeled from colored pencils. They ground sidewalk chalk to dust and blew it in her eyes, made tripwires from the strings of their toy guitars, perfected the art of delivering papercuts with construction paper.

There was nothing they couldn't use, couldn't weaponize. Stella cut her hair short, wore long sleeves even in summer, but still the list of her wounds grew. There was no bit of her soft flesh or exposed skin that was safe.

What little was left of her they'd wipe away in time. After all, they were still only boys. They were getting smarter, stronger, bigger. She thought about it whenever she put food on their plates, when she dropped them off at school, when she took them to the dentist for regular cleanings. All the good things she did for them, they'd turn against her in the end.

She tried to remember what she used to look like—before the ill-healed broken nose, the twisted posture from her wobbly left knee, the half eyebrow lost to a flying birthday candle. She used to be pretty, she thought, but her sons would never know that. She saw their mother in the mirror: a lumpy monster with bloodshot eyes and thinning hair. If they loved her at all, she couldn't see how.

But she told the boys she loved them often. More out of desperation than affection, for surely they must already know. If the warm meals and soft beds and bathing of dirty limbs and spoonful of medicine weren't enough proof, then there were these: the stretchmarks, the crutches, the welts, the scabs, the scars, her crooked fingers, the destruction of the body as a memoir of her motherhood.

She must love them, she thought, and sometimes said out loud, to take all this and come for more. Who would do that, but a mother?

SUCH A FUN AGE

K. S. Walker

"**W**hat are you reading?"

You look up from your book to the stranger who just eased onto the far end of *your* bench and then up to Evan on the merry-go-round and then back to the stranger. "Oh. It's a fantasy," you say, your eyes already searching the page for the sentence you left behind.

It takes a moment, but you settle back into a rhythm. You're ready to turn the page when the stranger in the red coat shifts. You can tell by the air between you that she's ready to ask another question. You surreptitiously peek at Evan, moving your head as little as possible, hoping that Talking-Tina can't tell that your eyes have left the book. Evan's round, brown face, smiling out of a hooded jacket, comes back into view. She still hasn't said anything. You finally exhale and lift a rough corner to turn it.

"What is he, five?" Interrupting-Ingrid rasps, nodding toward your child.

"No," you answer, without telling her that he's almost three because it's only white ladies who would mistake your barely-not-a-toddler for a child that much older, and she doesn't need to know his age, anyway.

You cross your right knee over your left, shifting your weight away from Playground-Pamela. You raise the paperback so that it almost touches your nose, but you can see Evan ease off the merry-go-round and tread through the woodchips toward the slide.

"Momma, look!" Evan croons from the top of the structure. In a blur of navy, he's whooshed down the slide. His two feet are barely on the ground before he's running back around toward the stairs. He could play here for hours. Without you. That's the point.

You deserve this. You push papers from nine to five. You put a vegetable on the plate at dinner *and* make the kid eat it.

You hang artwork. You kiss boo-boos. You hide. You seek. You bite your tongue until you taste blood when 'he's not *giving* you a hard time, it's just that he's *having* a hard time' and then read bedtime stories when all you really, really want? Is a second glass of Malbec. You're both the hero and the bad guy, and today? You even remembered to shower. You deserve a small moment that belongs to you and only you. Don't you? *Don't you?*

Satisfied that the kiddo is safely occupied, you lower your eyes. You'd kill to finish this scene. The playground drops away as magic-wielding half-men half-beasts roar into battle. You grip the book a little tighter, eyes scanning a little faster and—*Is she fucking serious right now?* Honestly, who still smokes anymore? And at a playground? Does she smoke around her own kids? Wait ... where are her kids?

You let your annoyance straighten your spine and give Lung-Cancer-Laura a pointed stink-eye. She winks through the nicotine haze. You arch around to bring the swing set and the jungle gym into view. They are just as empty as when you arrived.

"You know what I love about kids? They're just so *malleable*. You can shape them, craft them into anything. *Nothing* is impossible at this age." Is her voice really that scratchy or do you imagine it more so because you find her abrasive?

"Look, lady—" you start to say, turning back to establish some boundaries. It's what your therapist is always telling you to do, right? Only, Evan calls out to you.

"Momma ..." he says. And it's the same voice you hear from across the hall when he's talking in his sleep. It sounds like he could have murmured it against your ear, or it could be a whisper carried across the ocean. You look back to the slide. Then the merry-go-round that's still spinning.

If a ride spins and your child isn't on it, was he even there at all?

Panic levers you forward, causing your book to tumble into the woodchips. Anxiety claws at your chest, your throat. You circle the play structure in disbelief; you cannot reconcile that your child was *just* here, and now?

"Such a fun age," a voice behind you cackles, and you spin back toward the bench, but the Wicked One is gone, too.

Blinked into the folds.

There's the slowing creak of metal on metal. Wind rustles dead leaves across the playground. A noise so small escapes your throat, you can't be certain you made any sound at all.

DAVENING

Leonard Kress

And then I fall into a small depression, a hole that's shallow enough so I can still see the world over the edge. It's more like an indentation in the ground of my daily life, one I have to climb out of every day, several times, to accomplish the slightest task. It's exhausting at first, but I find that I can build up some muscular or psychic endurance, as if my day begins with a brisk run up a hillock or a twenty-minute session on a treadmill adjusted to a four-percent incline. After a few weeks, it seems normal enough, easier, of course, than waking up in the middle of the night to rock my baby back to sleep. Because this is surely the bigger challenge. The initial stages are easy: Pick up my bawling baby and hold her in my arms, her tiny head nestled between my chin and neck like a violin. Then slowly and deliberately lower myself into the rocking chair. This is a delicate stage because my baby is always about to enter a calm state, and if I jerk down too quickly into the seat, she'll wake up. This usually happens because it's a low and tiny seat, probably owned by the small old lady, the wife of the organist—the former inhabitants of this house. All those days and weeks of climbing out of my depression are helpful in this regard—my thigh muscles are more toned than they've ever been, and I view this lowering as a controlled squat. Once seated, the rocking begins, slow and rhythmic like all rocking, always leaning a little forward for reasons that I can only attribute to genetics. It's as though my rocking is actually some sort of *davening*, something I imagine my grandfather and his ancestors enacting, even though my limited exposure to religion and my father's total rejection of religion confuse matters. I've only seen Orthodox Jews *daven* in movies, and I've always been struck by the awkwardness of the gesture—compared to the svelte, sleek, controlled movements of yoga practitioners. I wonder, though, if they had prepared for this kind of rocking-back-and-forth prayer by doing squats—

making sure to bend their knees and not to lock them in place, which is what they all seemed to do. Or if they had allowed themselves to fall into the kind of mild depression that I often slip into, then they would learn to keep their knees loose as a way of preserving energy, making it easier to climb out of the hole so many times a day. But I suspect that their strict adherence to the Law made them view both depression and uncalled-for physical exertion as violating God's promise to them. I, on the other hand, think about mountaineers and their permanently bent knees, their perpetual ascent and descent. I have become a master, then, if not at prayer, then at getting my baby to sleep, itself a kind of prayer.

EDEN

Jami Nakamura Lin

A utumn
In the garden there was chard there, and there were dead there, and the frost had hit there, and the ground was hard.

You look at the white crackle in the soil—like mold, like chapped skin—and you think, *Nothing will ever come of this again.*

Spring
Only the dead keep rising.

"What's that?" our two-year-old asks, as we stamp around in the soil. She points at something round and beige poking through the weeds.

"Is that a Barbie hat?" my husband asks, but the tiny cap is embroidered with the Bass Pro logo, and I know. I yank out some weeds, brush away the dirt, and there it is: a mat of black hair growing underneath the cap, a pair of aviator glasses just barely visible through the dirt.

Like an errant carrot, my father is taking root in our garden.

"Did you put cardboard down last fall?" my husband asks, pulling out a clump of crabgrass. "Cardboard first, *then* the compost," he says. "That's how you keep the weeds back."

I did not do this. Last fall, grief kept me indoors. Drawn face, drawn shades. Now look: Creeping Charlie in all the corners, clumps of crabgrass, invasive flowers, expired fathers.

"Hi, Dad," I say, as I sprinkle lettuce seeds down a furrow. "Good growing, Dad," I say, as I transplant the tomatoes outdoors. Each week, more of him emerges. There's his nose, and the next week, his upper lip.

I try to cajole my daughter across the garden's chicken-wire fence. "Your Agon wants to see you. He'll be so surprised at how big you are!"

"No," she hollers, her O long as a hymn.

"Sorry, Dad," I say, after setting her up with a tablet in the hammock. He smiles beatifically but still does not speak. He looks like someone buried a bobblehead up to its neck—decapitated. Perhaps he needs more energy. Fish emulsion, mushroom compost. I wait impatiently for his voice to gather strength.

Summer

Dragging my daughter into the garden, I am knocked off-balance by her wiggling. We land hard in the dirt. Will she cry—she does not. "I want to go INSIDE," she says.

"We should say hi to Agon, since we're here," I say.

She shakes her head.

"Just one hi, then inside."

"Hi."

I grind up all his favorite foods—green grapes, chips, daikon soaked in sugar and shoyu—and pour them over his roots. He's grown up to his waist. His hand when I stroke it is the skin of a month-old potato. "Dad?" I say. "Dad?"

He still is not ripe enough to talk. It has been so long.

One evening my husband comes home to find her in the hammock on her tablet, jelly crumbs stuck to her thighs.

"Was she out here all day?" he asks. "Did you at least put on her sunscreen?"

Fall

During the hour of the ox, when the fabric between the living and the dead is thinnest, I look at the tops of his sports sandals coming through the earth. In the moonlight the weeds throw long shadows. I've given up on all the plants except my father; I've lost the plot.

But soon he will be fully emerged. And then what?

The thought of my father decaying with our kitchen scraps is enough to make me weep. I rub the tears on his ankles.

The next morning I swear his mouth is more ajar.

I plop her in the hammock, sit next to him, and think of

every sad thing. The last time he held her, when he lost his strength and slid down the wall. How he said, "Thank you for taking care of me." I smooth my tears on his face.

They are not enough.

I shut off her tablet. "No," she wails. I collect her tear with my thumb. "No," she says, when I carry her over the fence. A loose wire catches her kicking leg, and she whimpers.

"Sorry," I tell her, "sorry." I set her next to my father. "We need to cry," I say.

"Why?" she asks.

"It will help Agon," I say.

How his body was at the end, all his crocodile skin.

"Cry," I tell her, but she does not. "Cry," I say again. I hold her face up to my father's tiny one and hold her cheeks between my hands. "Cry," I say, holding her tighter than I ever have before. Nose to nose, mouth to mouth. "Cry," I tell my daughter, and finally, she does.

SIGHT, SOUND, SMELL, TASTE, AND TOUCH

Jamie Etheridge

This is how it looks: A slight blue cast beneath her tender skin. Or is that the moonlight? Her little eyes red and dimmed. And yet that same secret smile even when she cannot breathe. Her breath a noun when all I want is the verb. So I gray morning, coffee and Ventolin.

This is how it sounds: Sucked air whistling like a ghost down the alleys of her clouded, contracted lungs. Swollen, inaudible syllables, al'bu'te'rol whispered like a prayer, only I'm not in a church, but the white lights of the hospital corridor feel holy, spectral.

This is how it smells: Chemical breeze Prednisone scents the food. Sweat-cured sheets and bleach-washed corridors on midnight trips to the ER, eau d'vomit across the front of my shirt. I hold her, smell her coconut shampoo, baby powder, and the stink of a urine-soaked diaper, now leaking onto my pants.

This is how it tastes: Inflammation is warm and creamy like hot butter, then salty and medicinal. Parked just behind my teeth grows a fear I've never tasted before. Asthma a word I now eat with breakfast.

This is how it feels: Her unstoppable wheezing is a recurring nightmare. In it, I'm driving a car from the backseat careening along winding hills, veering near the cliff edge, over which I can see an ocean, sapphire and wild, beckoning. I struggle to steer. My arms stretch across the empty driver's seat, trying and failing, to reach her.

VOODOO

Christopher DeWan

You walk into your daughter's room. You wouldn't do this normally. You try very hard to respect her privacy, even when this sometimes causes you to wonder if you're being a bad or neglectful parent. The fact that you wonder means that you probably are not a bad or neglectful parent. But everyone has better days and worse days.

Her alarm clock is going off, and she's nowhere to be found, so you walk into her room, and that's when you see them: Two little dolls. Voodoo dolls of you and your wife.

"Maybe it's an art project," Janine says, when you tell her about it later that night. "She's always been kind of a strange girl."

The next day, while your daughter's at school, you sneak back into her room to have another look. But her desk is empty. You open the drawers and rummage through, careful not to make a sound, even though no one's home. But you don't see them. You check her dresser, filled with underwear that looks too lacy to belong to your little girl. You feel guilty going through her things. "Dad," she'd say, "what are you doing?" You're not sure what you'd answer.

As you pull up the comforter to look under the bed, your phone terrifies you by ringing.

"Hey. What's up?"

Janine has a migraine, came on suddenly. She's on her way home.

"I'll have a cold compress ready for you. That helps a little, right?"

Janine's firm depends on her, and she likes that, which means she works long days and then brings work home with her, too. Your own consulting business has been slow lately, and you find it's more satisfying to weed the garden and to cook elaborate meals than to power on your computer to drum up new clients.

You're chopping vegetables when Janine comes through the front door, and before you can ask how she is, she throws up on the foyer rug.

"Go to bed. I'll clean it up."

Your daughter comes home an hour later. "Eww, what are you cooking?"

"It's chicken stew. You like chicken stew."

"I'm vegetarian."

You had no idea your daughter was vegetarian. "Tell you what: I'll take the chicken out."

"Gross!"

You don't know how to ask if she's playing with voodoo dolls. You're not even sure "playing" is the operative verb. The dolls were made of sticks bound together with wire, and dressed in old Barbie clothes. What makes a voodoo doll a voodoo doll? What authenticity? You touch your head, feeling for pinpricks. You don't feel especially well, but you don't know if that's black magic or just the normal kind.

"Honey, can I talk to you about—?"

But she's already gone upstairs and closed her door.

It's unfair, isn't it, to pour so much hope into one's child? To ask them to be the flimsy vessel of so much expectation? We want all the things for our children that we never had—which means we're asking them to succeed where we ourselves have failed. Why can't we just simply love?

You knock on her door. "Can I come in?"

She's on her bed, doing what looks like homework.

"You know your mom's sick, right? Some kind of headache."

Your daughter pauses at this information, but gives no indication whether she herself has driven a hatpin into her mother's avatar brain.

"What are you working on?" you ask, when you notice the paper you assumed to be algebra is actually filled with unreadable symbols.

"It's cool," she answers. "It's like a secret code."

"Can you tell me what it says?"

"Then it wouldn't be secret."

You look at her, this little creature. You recognized her, you think, when she was three, when she was seven. She seemed like someone who could be a daughter of yours.

But lately you're not sure.

"You hungry? You want grilled cheese?"

She shakes her head and goes back to coding.

While you're washing dishes, you get a nosebleed. You watch the blood fall into the dishwater: The drops are slow to disperse. They hang between the suds and the enamel, floating wispy globes. Slowly they spread into thin red clouds, little sanguine genies offering you a chance to make a wish—but do it quick, before they disappear forever. You watch your blood floating in the sink, fading. There are so many things you could wish for. So many things.

A MURDER, A BIRTH, A CERTAIN KIND OF DEATH

Jennifer Fliss

S he can tell the time by the murder of crows overhead. Her breasts are leaking, and the cacophony of the corvids soothes the primitive part of her. The sound almost drowns out her baby's cries.

It's hot, so she and Sophie are on the back porch under an umbrella covered in bird shit on the outside and knit with spiderwebs on the underside. She thinks the burning waves of the sun might kill her sooner, but the energy it would require to crank the umbrella closed is beyond her capabilities, now two months since her baby slithered, goopy and covered in blue-white vernix, from her. A vile impression of a human, a human she was supposed to adore and nurture from the minute it could breathe.

One of the crows swoops down. It's the one she's been feeding peanuts to, the one who occasionally leaves her gifts. She can tell by the uneven molting and the feather that sticks out at the wrong angle. People think these birds all look the same, but they don't. They don't even have the same calls. If you listen and look closely, you'll know which one is yours. She has spent hours coaxing the birds, sharing her food, jumping at their call to run out and take care of them.

Then Sophie was born, and she didn't have time for all that. Didn't have time to shower, to call friends back, to eat more than English muffins out of the bag—not even toasted. She choked those down and then choked some more, and no one was there to offer CPR, so she died.

The crow landed on the back of a chair, bent its head knowingly at her. She acknowledged the bird with a slow nod. Looked over at Sophie bawling—god, her head hurt from all the wailing—and an image filled her mind's eye: A bird of prey pulling the child, her child, into parts, like a chicken, leaving behind a desiccated but silent thing. She shook the image from her head. She had always been the one—that one—where friends said, "You're so good with kids" and "You'll be a great mother!" and so on.

Instead, she was a monster. A brutal, broken mother-monster.

The crow took a cautious dinosaur-clawed step to the side and dove toward the baby car seat, where Sophie's bloody-heart-colored face puckered and spouted infant obscenities. In the face of her cries, the crow cawed, tilted its head, pecked at Sophie's chest, at her clothing.

She watched in interest. She felt the film that had dropped over her eyes weeks before wavering, lifting perhaps.

The crow hooked the baby blanket in its curved beak and tossed it aside, plucked at Sophie's wispy hair, and secured its beak on the neck of her onesie. Tugged.

Surely, Sophie would be too heavy, she thought. Surely, she should, what? Help the crow? Help the baby? Her crow? Her baby? She had to look away. She studied a stain on her shirt, brought it to her nose, sour-milk smell—she had soured. She had gone bad. She was rotten. *Don't drink me*, she thought.

The crow pushed its beak in further to get a better grip on Sophie, gave a big flap and rose, taking the infant with it.

She should stop it. She should shout, "No, not my baby!"

Lumbering under the weight, the crow was languid in the air, but still aloft. What a miracle to be able to carry such a weight and continue to fly.

She watched the bird skim the rhododendron—still not deadheaded and filled with the corpses of brownish-pink flowers. Through the juniper's craggy branches, up, up, up, and over the bigleaf maple. Her baby became smaller and smaller in the tranquil blue air, until the crow swooped and dipped and soared out of sight.

She lay back on the lounger, which was still damp from the previous night's rain. The wet seeped through her threadbare leggings. Her breasts—heavy with milk a second ago, gave a sharp protest and then lightened.

An hour later, she still sat there. At the base of the maple, she saw a shiver in the grass and peeled herself from her seat to inspect it. There, barely a few days old maybe, she found a crow chick, red-mouthed and blue-eyed like the sky. She scooped it up.

"I will call you Sophie," she said, and brought it inside, holding Sophie close to her body, warming it between her breasts. She found a dropper that had been used for baby aspirin, a shoebox she filled with decorative straw from a baby-shower gift.

When her husband came home, he asked how the day went.

"Great," she said. "Come say hello to your girl."

The murder moved elsewhere. The young monster-mother no longer heard their plaintive caws nor found on her doorstep the gifts of dead animals.

PHANTOMS

Diane Gottlieb

T he ghosts and I have never met a mirror we liked. Still, in the
barren hope of finding one that might show us what we want
to see, we stand in front of every surface that renders our reflection: any window, sheet of metal, pane of glass. Turning to the
left, we present our sides, our full cuts of meat, hands wisping
over bellies, ever so lightly, as if those bare brushes of fingers
against cloth, against skin, prayers with open palms, could make
even the slightest difference. We give ourselves up, an offering
of peace, of *please*, of *come on, now*. A sacrifice to the mirror gods,
we bring ourselves, our fatted calves, our pascal lambs. (We'd
bring our firstborn sons—we *would* offer our firstborn sons.)
Then, we turn our heads just enough to peer into that surface of
judgment, a vain search for the selves we'd be proud to call
"ours."

People say the measure of another can be found in the mirror. They say mirrors reflect the soul. They say mirrors don't lie.
We say, five more pounds. We say, worthless. We say: *fat.*

My daughter is two. Clad only in a diaper, she follows me
into the kitchen and stops directly in front of the tinted glass on
the oven door. It stands in line with her belly, her soft, baby belly, round and full. She turns to her side, places her chubby little
hands on that delicious, smooth belly and moves those hands
gently up and down. Just as she's seen me do, as I've seen my
mother do, as I imagine she saw her mother do, as we do, as we
do, and have done since the beginning of time.

In the Jewish tradition, when someone dies, the mourners
cover the mirrors in their homes for seven days. The purpose:
to mitigate distraction, discourage vanity. There's another reason, too. Covering mirrors keeps the ghosts away.

We don't keep our ghosts away.

We're mourners. We're loss. But our ghosts are alive in our
secrets.

My daughter is two. She peers into the glass on the oven door. For her reflection. She does not look straight-on but turns her body to the side.

People say ghosts creep into the nursery. They say ghosts travel through your genes. Sins revisit. Trauma flows in the blood. We say, there are too many secrets for us to carry alone. We say, our secrets weigh us down. We say, if we pass them along, *we'll never lose you.*

My daughter is two. She still giggles when she sees her reflection. She has not yet seen her ghost.

My mother's ghost. Her mother's ghost. They whisper in the wind. Call out through my cells. They're visitations in the bowl. In my vomit. Telling me *you're too big. You're too much.*

My daughter is two.

I lift her in my arms. Kiss her beautiful belly. Look at her velvet cheeks, her pink mouth, her nose. My eyes. They will be her mirror, as they sing to her softly. Spill this most precious secret: *You're enough. You're enough. You're enough.*

Diane would like to thank all her ghosts—especially her mother, whom she misses dearly and will always love fiercely.

THE SPECIFIC LENGTH OF SCARS

Melissa Bowers

While the rest of the world is desperate to avoid it, I know I will become my mother by the time I'm thirty-eight. There were always signs: Both of us allergic to citrus. Both of us only children. The voice no one else could hear, the one that began as an indiscernible rush of wind and appeared to each of us on the last day of first grade—toothless seven-year-olds in nearly identical school photos, one in black-and-white and one in color.

Whenever I confide in a friend, the friend brings up wrinkle cream. Or hair dye. Or that sentence she swore she'd never say, like *I'll give you a reason to cry* or *Because I said so,* and claims the exact same thing is happening to her.

I tell the grocery clerk as I thumb through paper-clipped wads of coupons just the way she used to: "Wow, I must be turning into my mother." I tell the mammographer as she squashes my breast in the machine like a flattening tube of dough, fresh scar shrieking. I tell the mail carrier. The neighbors. Everyone laughs and says, "Aren't we all turning into our parents?" and I imagine grabbing them by the shoulders and pressing my forehead flush to theirs and rasping, "You don't understand. I am *becoming* her."

To become my mother I will need to be a mother, though I worry I'm too far from maternal, at least in the way the world expects. I love painting, poetry, travel. Sleep and silence. Freedom. I love so many things that are not baby-shaped.

Granddad reminds me again about the divorce—the most recent fact he remembers—and I remind him again that children can exist without husbands. I spoon a bite of mushy food into his parched mouth the same way I will feed the future infant I'm not sure I want.

I change his underwear, saggy and stained. I put him to bed.

Neither diagnosis is a surprise.

One spirals toward death: "It's in your thyroid now," the doctor says gently, and the next word—*surgery*—starts gently, too, builds into a throbbing skull echo. This is exactly how it went with her. I look down at my lap and see my mother's knees.

One spirals toward birth: A pregnancy test. A man still nameless because I never asked, because he was a harmless face on a lonely night, because I choose to keep him that way.

The only news Granddad will hear is the good kind. *Good good good good good*, it chants, though my cells scream as they divide. I leave the bathroom and show him the stick, its tip soaked with urine. He stares at it with glazed eyes.

Three scars so far. She ended up with six. They are shaded in order of appearance: the gash beneath my breast a marbled ivory, the one on my neck a subdued pink, the cesarean slice new and raw and red. At night, in the loud dark, I sometimes can't tell which condition feels scariest: one with potential to overcome a body, or one with enough power to overcome an identity?

I lift the baby from the bassinet and kiss her hairline, all along the sweet, tender head made of fuzz and soft bones. Sway. Swollen milk ducts strain against the scar while Granddad calls repeatedly for more soup, and I'm not sure who most needs to be fed. One latched to my left nipple. One slurping from a spoon. Sway. Sway. *When is the last time you've eaten?* it asks, the tone different now. More familiar. I rummage through the fridge with one arm, the other still cradling the baby, but nothing is fresh. Everything is growing mold. It all grows mold eventually.

I yank the aging yellow fruit from the crisper, and the baby startles and detaches. I set her on the floor beside Granddad. A flicker of recognition on his face, a flash of real eye contact, before he calls me by my mother's name.

He is the only one who understands.

I used to watch her in the bathroom mirror, rubbing lemon pulp on her skin despite our allergy. She'd double over and breathe between clenched teeth and then keep going, anyway. *The juice lightens scars,* she says, so I cut the lemon into wedges. *Sometimes we do things even when we know they'll hurt.*

It stings at first. I cringe and gasp the way she taught me, but something isn't right. Her scar was longer. With a fingernail I dig and scratch, and Granddad calls for more soup, and the baby wails from the floor, and I sway and scratch and sway and scratch. I am already thirty-eight. Our wounds are not yet the same. *Just give one more inch,* she says, so I dig.

SHADOWS

Caroljean Gavin

Every night before I leave for my shift, my wife likes to make some kind of joke. "Don't bring one home with you! We're all out of shadow kibble!" Tonight it's "Don't bring one home with you! Those shadow leashes are slippery! I dropped ours behind the bed, and it disappeared!" She is so funny. So, so funny. Usually. Not with these jokes, though. I laugh anyway because I love her. She's trying. She's trying to pretend this is all normal.

I go in through the back door of the shelter, straight to the broom closet, fill up the yellow bucket, put on a fresh mop head, and drag myself over to the kennels. In the daytime, the place is buzzing with people looking for cute, young, nonaggressive, housebroken pups who don't require too much exercise. There are also the drop-offs, the surrendered, the abandoned, the lost and the found. Always more coming in than the shelter can hold. The dogs who go to sleep and don't wake up leave their shadows here. I absolutely hate my job, but if I don't clean up the shadows, they will stay and disturb the other dogs. Just their presence scares hopelessness into the new arrivals. I have to erase all traces of their lives to erase all traces of their deaths. I do not get paid enough for this shit.

The rottweiler's shadow is easy. He's huge and laying out across the middle of the floor. I don't think he's sleeping, even though his front paw is flickering a little with a twitch. When I bring the mop over his paws, he shakes out his ears. "I'm so sorry, buddy," I say, and I swipe the mop over his nose. He sneezes. I close my eyes and wipe the floor. Shadows don't have vocal cords. The dogs never whine.

The chihuahua circles around me, charges forward and springs back, over and over again. Territorial, but not that smart. "It's okay, honey," I say, as I spin the mop slowly around, knowing it will catch her while her eyes are fixed, just waiting for me to turn my back.

The pitbull is giving me a hard time. She is so playful. She tries to grab hold of the mop with her teeth, but of course her shadow teeth go right through it. It's okay. I can give her this. She's the last dog of the night, anyway, and it feels so good to play. I don't even remember to listen for the door.

"Who's there?"

Fuck.

"Samantha, is that you?"

If I say no, will it be funny? It doesn't matter, because before I can decide, Gwen is standing in front of me.

"Shit, Sam. Barb told me to call the cops if I saw you here again," Gwen says. The pitbull likes Gwen and runs up to her, licks her hand.

"I can't leave them like this," I say. "They're gone. They shouldn't be here anymore."

"I'm sorry," she tells me, "for everything that happened. I know you miss your job. I know it's been hard. But you have to go home. The shadows are fine. They're happy. They're not bothering anyone. Go home, Sam."

The pitbull butts her sweet shadow head against my leg. I wish I could take her with me, but I know she won't go. I know she'll stay forever in the place she fell asleep.

For one, I don't know how I'm going to break it to my wife. She hasn't been working, and at least one of us needs to have a job. But for another, I don't want to go back home. I don't want to see her rocking in that room, singing lullabies. What the hell am I going to say? "Hey, I'm back! Shadow diapers were buy one, get one free!" or "Oh, I was thinking, we need to hurry up and get on the list for shadow preschool." She will not laugh. Our life is not funny. And I will still hear it, too, the crying.

THE MERMAID'S EGGS

Keri Modrall Rinne

The mermaid, whose name was a sound no human could make, knew more about humans than they knew of her. Her long hair fell in heavy, reddish-purple hanks, exactly like the seaweed that clotted the tidepools where she plucked up sea urchins and crabs and crunched them between her teeth. She thought of how she would teach her children to pry open mussels with a well-placed limpet shell, blow bubbles underwater so they clustered and caught the sunlight, and her favorite thing: how to grasp something by the neck so it could not escape.

The mermaid's eggs had not yet hatched, and she watched her children's bodies grow day by day, shifting and twitching inside their leathery pillow-shaped sacks with a strand coiling at each corner. Another example of something humans did not know about her: her eggs were just like a shark's. She'd anchored the eggs using a length of her hair and a narrow braid of baleen.

This was her most vulnerable time and theirs. She didn't like to stay so long in the shallows. She longed for the soothing cold pressure and darkness of the depths. Days passed, and the mermaid's scaled spine was turning gummy as it was exposed to the air. She sucked a sculpin and huffed her silvery lips in annoyance when a rogue wave pushed her against the ragged side of a rock. She was so over this tidal zone.

She was trying to relax, letting her body move and sough with the tide, when she heard it. One of the stinking furry things that humans brought to the beach. It moved lightly enough, but she knew it brought filth on its hairy paws. It was not of this place. Then she heard something worse: the sliding crunch of a man's feet on the rocks where every inch held something living, something now crushed. She could always tell when it was a man. No poise or care, just destruction. He was too close. She could not untie her eggs and carry them to a safe place. She lay facedown and draped herself next to the pool, her own body camouflaged while her children were tethered, helpless.

She heard the heavy skid of the man's boots and smelled his sunscreen and sweat and some other sharp blend of chemicals that twisted into her like tiny hooks. She opened an eye and gazed at her children. Her daughter gazed back at her, and then they both watched as the man lowered his fat, dead-whale's hand and grasped the egg that contained her son. The egg came loose when the man tugged, and he brought it close to his face. The mermaid did not hesitate then—she rose and snatched the man's wrist. Her son in his egg fell with a small splash. She glanced down and then snaked a hand to the man's surprised face, pushing it into his mouth to silence him. She heard the dog coming back to investigate and felt the man surge.

"You think *this* creature can save you?" she whispered, laughter frothing.

Her hand whipped out and snatched the dog. Then she fell backward, down, pushing rapidly under the surface, feeling the relief of using the full strength of her tail to propel the three of them away from the foaming glare of the surface. She remembered another egg purse, a glimmering pearl of a baby inside, another foot pressing down before the mermaid could react. Not this time. This time it was like being given a gift. Two gifts. Like killing two fish with one spear.

Later, when the sun was half a sinking jellyfish, she swam back to her children and ran her fingers over the surface of her daughter's egg. The tiny thing opened her eyes, two bioluminescent orbs, and by their light, the mermaid saw her daughter point. Her son's egg was caught on the tip of a sea-star leg. The mermaid mother released it, cupping it once to her mouth before lovingly weaving the strands of the eggs together, securing them among a crust of barnacles. She felt a vibration shiver from her son's egg, and a fish grin stretched her mouth wide. She released a single bubble of joy and nestled down into the shifting sand to wait.

ICE ON THE WINGS

Jan Stinchcomb

I get to relive one day. That's all. For me, a crash ended everything, but the full range of trauma runs through our circle. Every form of loss. An assault stole one woman's child. For another, it was a cult. Disease. Suicide. Accidents. Plain old bad luck. There are endless ways to lose your baby.

We sit in the basement of the witch's house where we form an uneasy circle in our metal chairs. It looks like AA or some support group, but there is an unholy purpose lodged in our hearts. We are transgressing, going against God and nature.

"It's for a whole day," Becca would remind me whenever I got cold feet. "One tender day."

Becca has been a devotee for years, but she has never been chosen. There is one meeting a year, and the witch picks only one mother at a time. If she looks you in the eye, you are the winner. You get to have your child back for the day of your choice. Most women choose birthdays. Smart women remember quiet days so they can have hours of delicious, uninterrupted time. I dream of seaside vacations, story times, inside jokes.

"You have to state the complete date," Becca told me the first time she invited me to join the circle. "Day, month, year. Be careful. Memorize it."

"And it will be an exact duplicate of that day? Every detail will be the same?"

"Down to the frosting on the cake. Down to the towels at the hotel."

"You've spoken to past winners?" I ask her.

"Only one," she whispers. "We're not supposed to talk about this."

"Did they say what happened? Is it like a dream? Will the other family members remember it later?"

"Calm down. They won't remember anything. You, the mother, are the only one who will retain the experience. And that's as it should be."

"I don't know if I can lie to my husband."

"Don't you think he lies to you?"

I bristle but promise to come with her to the witch's house on the next full moon.

Now, I must choose the date. I look through all my pictures, something I haven't been able to do since the day everything changed. Do I even have a favorite age, a favorite memory? I settle on the day we got on the plane to move out here. Many women choose a day from toddlerhood, when they could still carry their child in their arms, but I am drawn to the one day I always blame. We should never have boarded that plane. We should have stayed where we were, and then we would have been able to keep our little family intact.

"Remember," Becca warns me as we approach the witch's house, "don't even think of pulling a fast one. You can't go back and change events. You must go through the day as it was. This is a chance to see your child again, nothing more."

"What happens if you don't follow the rules?"

"Why would you ask that?"

"Just tell me."

"You'll make things worse than they already are."

"Do you know anybody this has happened to?"

Becca purses her lips and refuses to answer. She shakes her head.

In my mind I have relived the airport scene a million times, how I grab my daughter's hand and march her out of there. Don't worry about the luggage. It doesn't matter. Our clothes can be replaced. Sometimes I change my airplane behavior. I don't let her leave my side. She isn't out of her seat when it happens.

Or I join her in the aisle.

It's okay if we die together. I'm easy to please.

"You're not going to do anything foolish, are you?" Becca asks when we are seated and waiting.

The doorknob turns, and a tremor passes through our crowd of hopefuls. The witch enters on one of the icy clouds I saw from the plane window that day.

"Are you?" Becca hisses. "Promise me!"

I don't say a word. The witch glides right up to me; her feet never touch the floor. She looks me in the eye, but it's her cruel sneer that surprises me.

She knows what I'm planning before I name the date.

And I can taste the sweetness before the harrowing plunge.

PLANT MOTHER

DW McKinney

Egan adjusted the rucksack on her shoulders as she stepped into the backyard. "Gotta say goodbye to my baby," she said.

Dust caked the patio furniture. The upholstery was threadbare where dirt had settled the longest. The yard was barren, except for the lone tree rising from the cracked ground. Its branches twisted upward. At its base was a blanket Egan had knitted for Ara.

Egan was ecstatic when Ara was born. She delighted in the idea that her daughter would live in the home Egan, her mother, and her grandmother had lived in. It was family land. A legacy they would steward for countless generations. Few enjoyed this privilege. But as soon as Ara could speak, she wanted to know, "When?" *When were they moving? When would they buy a new house? When would their life be less boring?*

Egan had asked her daughter, then a small child, why she wanted to leave behind a place that was set aside just for her.

"Just 'cause," Ara responded. Dissatisfaction flowed through her, but she couldn't articulate why.

Thinking of her daughter, Egan caressed the tree trunk. If Ara had given her a convincing answer, would Egan have considered it? Would she have moved then instead of now?

Would it have made a difference? she thought.

Egan picked up the blanket and clutched it to her chest. There were no right answers. A gust of wind swept across the yard. She flinched from the memory it brought more than from the corrosive dust it carried with it.

During one windy afternoon, Ara had stood outside in a gust of swirling dust and trash, laughing. It took two pints of their water rations to clean Ara's face and hair, but yellow bead-sized pods still clung to Ara's coils.

Seeds? Egan thought.

It had been so long since she'd seen viable ones. Peering closer, Egan discovered that Ara's hair threaded the seeds as if they were a lock and key. Egan wanted to cut the seeds out then, but Ara resisted.

"Only people with dust sickness get haircuts!" she howled.

This was untrue, but Egan relented. She was sure the seeds would fall out with time.

Instead, the seeds grew until tiny roots snaked from their round bodies and strangled Ara's hair. Within a week, flora blossomed. Ara attended secondary school with a vibrant flower crown like a twentieth-century maiden. Ara loved the attention. The novelty rewarded her with gifts from strangers and an excuse to behave however she wanted. Egan worried. She had been on this dying rock long enough to know that such oddities only carried ill results and unwanted consequences. While Ara slept, Egan tried to cut the blooms. Better to halt the tragedy and deal with the pain in the aftermath. But the stems only thickened as Egan snipped at them.

When the plant matter weighed down Ara's head so that she walked with a hunch and complained of headaches, Egan kept Ara home from school. They stopped venturing out in public. When a sapling emerged from her scalp, Ara could only lift her head with assistance. Egan and Ara spent their days in the backyard, lying on Ara's baby blanket.

"Mama, I don't want to die," Ara whispered one evening. Roots wreathed her head. They tightened as she stared at the velvet sky.

"No one's dying," Egan murmured. "I'm your mother. It's my job to keep you alive."

Egan fell asleep as her daughter counted the stars. When Egan woke, Ara was gone. A tree was in her place. Its smooth trunk had Ara's body. The faint jut of hips and the rise in her chest. Ara's face was clear in the fresh, green bark. Egan spent hours staring at her daughter's expression. She couldn't decide if Ara's face were twisted in agony or excitement.

The bark, now thickened and rough, made it difficult for Egan to locate the ridges that had once been fluttering eyelids and a mischievous smile. Finding them, she pressed her forehead to the tree trunk. Egan cradled Ara's oaken face and nuzzled the bump of nose.

"You will live," she whispered.

Then Egan reached up and pulled on a branch that had once been her daughter's right arm. She wiggled it back and forth until it gave with a wet snap. She swaddled the branch inside the baby blanket, then stuffed it in her rucksack. Egan would carry the branch with her. It would grow wherever she planted it.

BLUE MAMA

Emma Brewer

Without thinking too deeply about it, we presume ourselves to be adequate parents. The baseline assumption is that we would do anything for the babies; we would fight, we would kill. Tonight somehow they outnumber us, although there are still two of them. The one who was born first has learned to escape his crib and howls for his twin to join him; the smaller twin rages to be let out. It's been three hours of bedtime, and we have given up. We're crouched on the floor in our room, staring into the baby monitor's small window, where the twins appear as if in the bottom of a fish tank: murky, grayscale, dull but for the flashes of eyes as they scream. This is when we see her in the monitor. We see her body, her drifting hair, the billowing arms, each one reaching for a twin's mouth. She's between the cribs, a cloudy heart between cages.

We've always understood ourselves to be proper parents, quick in a catastrophe, selfless. Maybe we can blame the day we've had. Because I spent today assisting that one surgeon who hates me, and after we removed a six-pound mass from a sleeping golden retriever, and I—swiftly, sublimely—stitched the incision, he whispered, "Think fast," and slipped the tumor into my arms and watched me drop it, watched the flecks of blood smatter while it wobbled at my feet. And you, arriving at yet another job interview, realized you'd worn your sneakers and scrambled to buy new, unaffordable dress shoes and—panicked, sweating—threw your own shoes into a dumpster outside the interview. And of course, of course, they were already gone when you went digging for them after.

We believe, we have faith, that we are sufficient parents, and we've spent the evening laughing at our failures while negotiating pieces of nourishment into the babies' mouths and then our own, while somewhere deep in ourselves a light shutters, a sun darkens, bones prickle in the sockets. We see her at the same time. Through the crackling of the monitor, we hear our younger twin say, "Blue," and our older twin say, "Mama." We see her reach for their faces, and what happens is a pause.

Inside the pause we recognize each other. The pause is prolonged by each of us witnessing the other one pause. That horror drifting over our children's bodies could be a demon thirsty for innocents, could be a witch with a pair of wicked changelings, could be an apparition born of shared delirium. She may be stronger than we are; she may lack our feeble need for rest and protein, our shameful limits; she may want nothing more than to draw from an inhuman wellspring of patience and sing our children to sleep. And you and I, we hold our breath to see what will happen, to find out if the ghost haunting our nursery is a better parent than we are. We take a long, terrible moment, before pelting to the room, before flooding it with light and sound.

EACH DROPLET OF BLOOD

K. C. Mead-Brewer

If it were as simple as pricking her finger and allowing each droplet of blood to land in the form of a baby, she would still not want children. Yet here is this little child, a nephew standing before her, announcing that his hair is full of lice. She could shave him bald, burn the house to the ground. He's never seen a firetruck. Okay, listen. It isn't her fault that her parents left their home so vulnerable to her, leaving her to care for this grandchild while they're away. It isn't her fault the boy's father is nowhere to be found, or that the mother was never here to begin with. He could almost be an orphan, she supposes. The kind from a fairytale. Even his eyes, look at them—wide as a princess'. The boy gazes up at her with those eyes and, to her horror, the pits of them, so deep and so dark, they begin to *rustle*. Not eyes at all, but teeming buttons of lice. No, absolutely not; she blinks and blinks. It's only tears, obviously. "Oh, don't cry," she says, "please don't cry. We'll get the lice taken care of, I promise." But it's too late. He saw the disgust in her. He clutches his small hands to his heart, all six of them, as if drawing a baby in closer. "What do you mean? Who will take care of them?" And good god. The question stretches her skin too tight. That he could misunderstand her so. That he could feel the parasite needing him, crawling all over him, making him itch and bleed and lonely and gross, and still, and yet. Who will take care of them?

ORDER UP

Joanna Theiss

S ummer in our new neighborhood meant construction, build-
ings raised to welcome hurricane season. My mother-in-law,
Alice, and I were lolling on beach chairs, watching a yellow
earthmover jerk over a bare plot of land.

"No cravings?" Alice asked, eying my belly like a hungry
crow.

"No. I feel great," I said. When Alice didn't reply, I lowered
my feet to the bleached concrete. "Does that mean something's
wrong, do you think?"

Alice patted my knee. "It's early yet."

I sat back, adjusting my shirt over my growing belly, breathing in time to the thudding of steel against rock, of the up-tempo
warning of a truck in reverse.

Andy was at a worksite when you sought escape.

During my out-breaths, I glimpsed Alice's fluffy bedroom
slippers pressed under the closed bedroom door. She'd been
there since the first contraction, calling out mindless, minimiz-
ing instructions.

Birthing you was nothing like the heaving, groaning messi-
ness of pushing out a live infant. Nothing like what Alice was
describing.

A mere plop, and you were there.

You were perfect, immaculately accurate. You fit in the palm
of my hand, tan with gentle, burgundy freckles. I cupped you
and felt your heat press into my skin.

"What's going on?"

"Go away."

"I can help, if you'd let me in. I've been through this before."

Alice couldn't help, hadn't been through this before. No one had, it seemed, because on this question, the Internet was binary. There were instructions for how to hatch a bird, and instructions for how to birth a baby. The decision tree did not include a third option, that of a human—I've always thought of myself as human—delivering an egg.

Alice did not leave. She was a sandblaster, wearing me down.

When I tried to explain, she said, "Like a chicken's? Or more like an ostrich egg?"

"Neither," I called back. Worried about keeping you warm, I snapped off the air conditioner buzzing in the window. "Can you bring it?"

Two hours later, your grandmother's reply was the thud of a box hitting hardwood. "No offense, but I don't think you need an incubator. I think you need a therapist."

I was brooding, impatient. To distract myself, I tended you. I changed your chips. I turned you. It was the seventh day, when the farmwoman online recommended that I candle you to find out whether you lived within your shell. Alice brought the expensive light I'd asked for, but I didn't like how she lingered after dropping it off. Her voice was blackberry sweet, provoking Andy, running her nails across my door.

"Postpartum happens with miscarriages, too, you know."

"I keep telling you, Ma, it wasn't a miscarriage. She's got something in there."

Alice's voice rose. "You're her husband. You need to shake some sense into her. She's … scrambled."

If I hadn't hardened toward him already, Andy's appreciative laugh would have curdled me.

When a hen begins laying, she may leave a little blood behind, smearing her baby's shell, but she will not leak blood on her bedsheets. The bleeding will not last for weeks.

I rested my cheek against the cool of the door, chewing the heat of the room, forgetting whether I'd turned you yet. Without the air conditioner, with your incubator humming at an ideal 100.5 degrees Fahrenheit, I was radiating, iridescent with heat.

"What have you been doing in the bathroom? It looks like someone died."

When I told him about the blood, Andy sounded worried for the first time since your delivery. He said that if I didn't go to the doctor, he'd break down the door.

"But it's nearly Hatch Day," I choked out, through a mouthful of feathers.

A broody hen will peck and scratch at the hands that reach into her nest and take away her eggs. But given the weight difference between a hen and a man, the fact that a man could wring her neck as easily as turning a screw, she has no real choice.

When I came home from the disbelieving doctor, the house smelled of breakfast. Unmistakable smells, of butter sliding across a heated nonstick pan, of creamy white albumen, firming above the gas flame. Of bubbling yellow yolk.

Alice and Andy, on either side of a pan. She, holding the spatula. He, sprinkling salt on a single egg.

Broody hens will peck and scratch. Broody mothers, watching their baby fry, will crack.

DARRELL

Eric Scot Tryon

In the eighth grade, Ms. Whipple gave each of us an egg. Told us to care for it like our own child. Feedings, sleep schedules, bathing and playtime, it was all to be documented. But most importantly, above all else: "Don't break the egg." Whoever could keep their child alive the longest got to pick the cake for the end-of-the-year party. Students came in daily with a sticky mess in their tissue box or simply emptyhanded and apologetic. Ms. Whipple kept count on the white board: "Dead Children," it read. The total ran up at a steady pace like the *Now Serving* ticker at an Italian deli.

The assignment was surely aimed at scaring us into never having sex, but that wasn't on my radar yet, anyway. I took the assignment seriously. While other kids named their children Eggs Benedict Cumberbatch, Yolk-O Ono, Egg Sheeran, I named mine after my father: Darrell. My child was hard as a fingernail, yet still thin as an eyelid, fragile and delicate, and I promised not to break him.

I ended up choosing carrot cake at the end-of-the-year party. My classmates were none too pleased, but Mom said it was my father's favorite. And then school let out and summer began, but I continued to care for Darrell. I washed him daily with room-temperature water and a soft hand towel. I read him haiku. I built a bed out of a shoebox, stuffed it with cotton balls, marshmallows, and triple-ply toilet paper.

High school came and went. But Darrell remained. Four years of missing parties, school dances, and football games. But what did that matter when you're trying to keep a child alive? I sang to him every night before bed, old Beatles' songs. Mom said they were my father's favorite. While other boys were pumping kegs in backyard parties, I hummed "Yesterday" to Darrell as we drifted off to sleep. And while other boys were struggling to undo bras in the cramped back seats of cars, my index finger caressed the smooth, rounded shell, vowing to be a good father. A better father.

Eggshells are actually not as smooth as one might think. They are mapped with tiny bumps and imperfections caused by a calcium-to-phosphorus imbalance. And by the time I graduated college, I knew the grainy topography of Darrell better than I knew my own hands. I spent every waking moment, and even the sleeping ones, worrying about how long I could keep this up. How long could I keep that paper-thin shell from cracking? Sometimes just transferring him from his cotton-ball bed to the bubblewrap insulation of our to-go container, I expected him to burst in my cupped hands, exploding into a yellow, sticky goo, forever ruined. Eggs are not built to stay whole.

I was thirty-two and living in a studio in San Diego when it happened. It had been two decades since Ms. Whipple handed Darrell to me, looked me in the eye, and said, "Don't break the egg." Teachers never expected much from me. And it wasn't an earthquake or a bar fight or a car accident. I was simply watching *Wheel of Fortune* and doing a crossword puzzle while a microwave dinner cooled. Darrell sat in a small tissue box on the TV tray. My hand brushed the box ever so slightly as I reached for a glass of water. That's all it took. A miscalculation of centimeters.

Darrell flipped end over end and landed on the hardwood with a wet splat. My breath caught and petrified in my chest. The TV crowd applauded the contestant who correctly guessed the letter T.

But when I looked down, I didn't see a shattered white eggshell and a runny sticky mess of oozing yolk. Instead, there was a heart the size of my fist. Purple and red, meaty and bloody. The way I imagined a cow's heart. Veins and capillaries, torn and frayed, stuck out like cockeyed guitar strings. There was nothing romantic or classic about it. It was wet and messy, and as it pumped and pulsated, blood spurted out of large arteries and valves. My stomach lurched at the sight and the rancid smell. But the rhythm. The timing of its beat was oddly familiar, comforting even, like a rhythm I had known my whole life, a rhythm much bigger than me.

AFTER-HOURS BABY

Rebecca Ackermann

My daughter has night terrors. I spring awake at the sound of a bat flapping and shrieking in her room. Her little legs have transformed into wings beating against the walls, her fists now claws tearing at her own skin, at mine, too, when I draw close.

"Get me out of here!" she screams. "Mommy, let me out of here!"

And all I can do is sit beside her, a rocky ledge along the side of her bed, keeping her from falling as she pushes against me, begging to be free.

My daughter has night funnies. I emerge from a dream to the cackle of a Borscht Belt comedian across the hall, punchlines landing with a guttural thud. Her timing is innate, her cadence a waltz with expectations and surprise.

"Take my mother, pleaaaase!" she booms. "One banana is not enough, three is a bunch too far!"

All I can do is be her audience, knees against my chest on the fuzzy rug I picked out for her room, as she finds her laughs from the row behind me.

My daughter has night theories. I stir at whispers behind her door of equations that span universes, crossing into alien dimensions. When I peek inside, she is standing on her bed drawing figures in the air, yellow-white eyebrows gathered in concentration.

"If I move this number here, I can travel to Pluto tonight," she mutters. "I can visit the babies and mommies who came before and be back by breakfast."

All I can do is try not to obscure the invisible calculations between us, watch and wait for her to return to me, the body that made her but cannot contain her anymore.

AN UNUSUAL REQUEST FROM EIGHT-YEAR-OLD HENRY

Veronica Montes

A t a shop in Montecito, Henry points to a Pierrot mask made of thin porcelain.

"This?" his parents ask. They dislodge it gently from its tenuous perch inside a French armoire. One eyebrow is arched higher than the other, the lips are red like cinnamon candy. "Doesn't this teardrop make it too sad?"

"Perhaps it's a happy tear," Henry says. He touches it with the tip of his index finger. "I'd like this, please."

Neither could resist the charm of Henry's manners; his politesse had long functioned as a kind of magic. They had raised him this way, of course, but many of their friends had done the same with their own children and enjoyed no lasting results. Henry found comfort in etiquette, in its rules and usually dependable results. There had been times, of course, when courtesy betrayed him, and rough kids called him names, locked him in the custodian's closet, squeezed glue into his backpack. His parents labeled these incidents "anomalies" and did not dwell on them.

Henry wore the mask throughout the drive home, occasionally frightening passengers in other cars.

"You shouldn't do that," his father cautioned after a few hours. "You're liable to cause an accident."

"I'm sorry," Henry answered. He slid down in his seat so he was no longer visible to the outside world. "Will you play that *Cinderella* music please, Mother? '*La Cener ...*' something?" His voice was muffled behind the mask, so he repeated himself until his parents understood.

"It's '*La Cen-er-en-to-la*,'" his mother said.

"Okay, thank you." He yawned.

"Do you remember the story of this opera?"

"Yes," said Henry. "It's like regular *Cinderella*, but the prince is in disguise, and there's no glass shoe. It's a bracelet, instead."

"Exactly right," his mother said. "It was such a topsy-turvy romp!" She turned to smile at Henry, but he had fallen asleep, the mask secure over his face.

After five days of their son's continuous mask-wearing, Henry's mother and father consulted the Internet, their library of parenting books, Henry's pediatrician, and their college friend's father, a renowned psychologist who was, frankly, no help at all. The consensus was to let Henry be: he was not, after all, harming himself or anyone else.

On the tenth night, they could bear it no longer. Together, they approached Henry as he sat curled up in a corner of the family-room sofa playing a word-search game on his iPad. They had discussed their tack and decided a jocular tone would be best.

"Buddy," his father said, "I miss your face!" He sat down beside Henry. "Do you have a full beard under there?"

His mother laughed, perhaps a little too loudly. "Let's take a look," she said. When she reached for the Pierrot mask, it cracked clean in half to reveal the startled face of a small girl. Henry's mother backed away, her hands over her mouth.

"I didn't mean to scare you," the girl whispered.

"Where is Henry?" said Henry's parents. They said it together, like the twins in that Kubrick film.

"I'm not sure." She rubbed her eyes and blinked several times. "Is that okay?"

"What do you mean, 'you're not sure?'"

The girl resumed her game then, no longer inclined to speak. The man and woman brought her milk and some peanut butter crackers, and then retreated to their bedroom. They opened their door intermittently to see if anything had changed on the couch.

After the third time of them peeking, the girl said, "It's still just me. And if I'm being honest, I don't think Henry will be back."

The man remained in the bedroom ...

(He would, in fact, keep his distance for many months, observing with fascination the way that Henry hovered like a nimbus over the girl's hands and the rise of her cowlick. "Do you see?" his wife would whisper. "Our child isn't gone, per se. Our child was always *this* child." He could see, the man could *almost* see, but he would persist in his gloom until one morning when it occurred to him that his extended sorrow could be considered a breach in etiquette and thus frowned upon by the polite child he had loved so dearly and, possibly, by the one who was waiting, with saintly patience, for a father.)

... but the woman ventured out. "Are you sure?"

"Pretty sure."

"Can I search for some words, too?"

"Of course. Come sit beside me."

The woman did as she was told, and the child leaned against her, warm and familiar.

WHITE LYE

Barlow Adams

M y son asks me to tell him about the first time I saw someone die.

He's really asking what it will be like if I die.

I tell him about Tiffany, my roommate in my first hospital, who had cystic fibrosis. How she let me try the pulmonary vest she wore that beat fluid out of her lungs by playing drums on her chest. How she loved ice skating, so I pretended to, as well, even though I couldn't manage rollerblades. The way they let us push our beds together so we would be less afraid.

I tell about her waking that night and grabbing my hand, smiling as if she had a happy secret to share before closing her eyes and drifting off forever.

My son finds peace in the story. In the thought of me drifting off with a knowing smile. It's an incredible tale.

Like my love of ice skating, it's a lie. As are all stories that sick parents tell their kids.

A blood clot in Tiffany's leg traveled to her lungs. She woke me by digging her nails into my wrist, eyes wide with terror and pain. She tried to speak, but the mucus was thick from sleeping on her back, and all she managed was a gurgle. My scream woke our moms, who were sleeping in chairs nearby. The crash cart rushed in. Tiffany's mom cried. Her daughter didn't make another sound.

What would a story like that do for my son? For his terrible fixation on my potential expiration?

When I'm finished with my lie, he tells me I'm brave. He's repeating what others have said. What everyone says. It makes me think of a lie by omission buried in my original fabrication. Tiffany was the first person I saw die. But not the first person I heard.

I was six. We were on vacation in West Virginia, driving around the mountains, listening to the truckers on my father's

CB radio in Mom's Oldsmobile Cutlass, the wide body of that boat on wheels sailing the trailer-park seas where my dad grew up. Their coded language seemed mystical, and their nuanced communication kept the dirty parts indecipherable to me and my mom. A hidden delight to my father—an escape within a vacation.

I got enough, however, to understand when one of the truckers came on the radio saying his brakes had gone out. He spent minutes communicating with the other big rigs, his voice calm and steady. Together they herded the cars and blocked off the roads to create a safe lane for the speeding eighteen-wheeler to ensure no one got hurt. Entrapped in the caravan, we saw the truck blaze by.

Going downhill with that weight, fate and momentum competed hungrily for the driver's life. The other truckers encouraged him, but the man knew. Had known for miles. He conducted his own dirge through that crackling CB, his rich molasses accent punctuated by blasts of his rig's deafening horn.

Just before he hit the guardrail, he said, "Tell my kids I love them."

The ordeal took so long that the police arrived before we did. By the time we reached the scene, the mountains were awash with emergency lights. We stopped the car and looked over the hill like visitors paying respect at a funeral. The truck was hundreds of feet down, crumpled like a can from multiple impacts, its contents spread across the mountainside.

He'd been hauling lye. It looked like snow. Winter in July. Picturesque and peaceful, the vehicle so small from that height it seemed like a broken toy train under a Christmas tree, nestled in powder.

My parents called him a hero. We talked about him for years. He became a symbol of sacrifice and courage. Reality blending into myth—the man illuminated like a saint against that white background.

I never tell my son this story. It took people calling me a hero for me to question it. To wonder about his brakes. The way he hit that guardrail, straight-on, his calm, resigned voice giving instructions on the radio. A final stoic message for his children. Was it possible to be so brave? So selfless? Or was his story, his legend, the biggest, sweetest knowing smile he could manage?

I think of my son staring down that hillside, and I grow fearful of the day he can pick apart my stories.

THE GIRL IN MY DAUGHTER'S ROOM

Madeline Anthes

The first time my daughter told me about the little girl in her room, I knew whom she was seeing.

"She's cold," Millie said.

I know, I wanted to tell her. *I know. The house is always cold when she's here.* Instead, I told her what we always tell children when they're scared at night. "You're safe. Mommy's here."

I crawled onto the bed with her and held my girl. Her night-light cast a blue glow over the room as she fell asleep.

When I left, I walked past the little form of a child hunched near the doorway and tried not to look.

We were happy and wanted a child. We had Millie, and it was easy, so I foolishly assumed it would stay easy. My body refused to give us another.

I wanted to defy the odds.

Marriages that experience a miscarriage are 22 percent more likely to divorce.

I don't understand statistics. Did we have a 100-percent shot at staying together, but then our first miscarriage reduced this to 78 percent? And after the second and the third, were we depleted to 34 percent?

I don't think statistics work that way. But things changed after every loss. I wasn't a woman he loved, capable of bearing life and surviving pain. I was the thing that hurt him over and over again.

Marriages that experience stillbirth are 40 percent more likely to divorce.

When we lost our last, a girl we named Kimmy, at 28 weeks, did that lower our chances even more? That gave us a -6 percent chance of surviving. Of course he left.

I found Millie piling blankets in the corner of the room.

"She's cold," Millie said.

Her room was frigid. I wondered then if I should just tell her. *I see her.*

Millie was only eight. Old enough to care for herself. But her mind was still flexible, able to create reality from imagination. I didn't want to confuse her.

"She's not real," I told her again.

Millie looked up at me, the same round eyes as her sister. "She said you'd say that."

I'd started seeing Kimmy a few months after her stillbirth. The visitors were gone. The casseroles stopped arriving. My mother stopped calling. Everyone was tired of the grief routine—how many times could we all go through this?

As everyone else forgot, I couldn't let go of the girl who could have been.

My husband was tired of my tears, my constant need, my hypotheticals. *Would they have looked alike? Would she have been a good sleeper? Would they have been friends?*

I told him how I saw Kimmy in our house. He said I needed more help than he could give me.

What are the odds of getting to see your child after they pass? What are the statistics of mothers who are hollowed out by the deaths of their children, only to see the one thing that would make them feel whole again?

I used to try to pick her up, try to hold her. But each time I drew too near and spoke to her, each time I looked directly into my daughter's eyes, she melted away in front of me.

I learned to keep my distance. Knowing she was there would

have to be enough.

But Millie could look at her, talk to her. It felt unfair that they could share something that I so desperately wanted. Millie went on as though this were all totally normal. She asked no questions. I should have been concerned, but I was relieved that I didn't have to explain.

I supposed I should try to bury Kimmy—metaphorically or physically. Isn't that how you vanquish ghosts? How could I vanquish the girl I'd always love?

Then one night I sat up in bed, finding two forms standing in my doorway. My gaze bounced between them—their matching eyes and similar smile. They looked like twins as they stood hand in hand.

"We're so cold," Millie said.

Kimmy giggled a laugh that echoed through my chest. The room was freezing.

I peeled back my sheets, and the girls climbed in. I tucked them in, my hand finally, finally, feeling Kimmy's solid back as I smoothed her hair, and watched them fall asleep next to each other. It was just how I'd always imagined—my two girls with me, at last.

In the morning, Kimmy was gone. I was still cold.

ELEVEN

Meagan Johanson

The seal skin hung slack, still dripping, in his daughter's closet. Stephen could see the strange drape of it from where he stood by her bed for goodnights. A slow trickle of water made its way outward, carefully catching the bedside light.

His wife was back, for a moment.

"The monsters, Dad?"

Nella still asked—although she was almost eleven. And he'd creak the floorboards, look under the bed. Into her hope chest of treasured beach stones and shells.

And inside the closet, of course.

The pelt was silk soft, like always, beneath the longing glance of his palms. He pulled it into his face, inhaled. It had been another long month between moons since he'd last seen Caitlin—and over a year since he'd given her selkie skin back.

Love isn't a trap, he'd told her. He wanted to believe this.

He searched for Caitlin's scent on the fur, but it was all brine, all beast and sea.

"No monsters," Stephen replied, like always—closing the door, sitting down on the edge of Nella's bed, scanning her face for some change. New teeth. Whiskers. Sloughing. He brushed a lock of hair from her forehead. Brown curls, like his.

"Can we go swimming tomorrow? I'm old enough."

"We'll see." He turned off the light and kissed her cheek, still hairless and smooth. Still human.

"Mom would let me."

Outside the window, the void of the ocean found the shore, hushing and rocking and trying again, like any good mother would.

"How is Nella?" Caitlin asked. Her neck was still damp from the shower, and she smelled sweet, like the pink shampoo.

Stephen clung to this part: the reunion, however short it would be. "She's happy. Loves middle school. A brand new world, wide halls and swear words. She's in advanced math. Choir, too. Sings all day, like you used to."

He took out two mugs, two teabags. Peppermint. Caitlin's favorite. The heater clicked on, hummed out the heat. The kettle hissed.

"Stephen, you know what I mean." Caitlin wrapped her arms around him from behind, as he stood at the stove.

"She wants to paint her room. Navy or teal, anything but pink. She asked me last week for lip gloss."

"She's growing up. It happens."

Stephen's chin dropped to his chest. "We're going to the beach tomorrow, for your birthday. She's asked all summer long to go swimming. What if she's—"

"—like me?"

"And me, a goddamn werewolf, waiting for the full moon each month."

Caitlin leaned her cheek into the nook of his shoulder blades, trailed her hands down his arms to loosen his fists, as the kettle founds its voice.

Nella's eyes stayed on the ocean as he lifted the steaming pot from the propane burner.

As he piled crab, lobster, potatoes, corn, fragrant and high on paper plates.

As he cut slices from the cake: *Happy Birthday Mom: We Miss You.*

"It's not a real birthday, anyways," Nella muttered, nudging a forkful of potato, leaning down to gather a shell from the sand. The strap of her swimsuit peeked out from her shirt, hopeful and bright against her skin.

"I just don't want you to forget your mom."

"Do you think I'd forget you?"

She brushed sand off her legs. A baby's cry broke the quiet that followed. At another picnic table nearby, a family packed up gear, the September evening settling in. The woman swayed and sung to her baby, the breeze carrying a lullaby Stephen knew well.

He had no choice.

He wanted to believe this.

"Okay Nella-Bell: I give."

Her shoulders straightened. Her eyes widened.

"You can paint your room. I don't care what color. And, if you finish your dinner—"

She picked up a crab leg.

"—you can go swimming."

Nella bit off the end of the leg—crimson shell and all—and chewed, the sounds of bones cracking, mountains crumbling, earth splitting. She swallowed, then took another motley mouthful.

Stephen's lips trembled, as he brought a corn cob to his mouth. "To Mom."

"To Mom," she replied, tearing through a lobster tail with a grin, wide and real and new.

He watched as the other family wound up the sandy path toward the road, and left.

In the setting sun, Nella turned quicksilver, as sure as a fish in the water. She rose from the horizon to wave, before diving back beneath the hush of the surf.

He couldn't see the moon. But he howled, anyway.

PACKING UP MY SON'S CHILDHOOD

Carol Scheina

On Thursday, I find the molted remains of my son's childhood crumpled on the bathroom floor, like a dirty shirt shoved into a corner, thin and wrinkled and seemingly far too small. Noah has slipped out of childhood like a snake shedding its skin.

I find him in the kitchen, his fresh teenage skin glistening in that baby-glow way with which he started out every other stage of his life. It won't last. The acne and attitude will soon arrive. I resist the urge to touch the fresh skin, knowing it will embarrass him. He's not a child anymore.

Noah pulls a juice carton from the fridge, and not for the first time, I'm thankful that he's tall enough now to reach the top shelf. No more asking Mommy a hundred times a day for juice or a snack he'd give two nibbles before declaring complete and utter fullness.

He takes a swig directly from the carton.

"Can't you use a cup?" I ask. "We all drink from that same container, you know." How many times will I have to remind my teenager?

He rolls his eyes at me—already performing the movement with mastery—as I grab a gallon-sized Ziploc bag from the pantry and return to the bathroom.

Noah's childhood feels sticky on my hands, reminiscent of lollipops and blobs of ice cream that no number of napkins will wipe off. A section smells of dried pee on bedsheets, the ammonia scent stinging my nose. And dirt. So much dirt. The kind that cements itself under fingernails after digging holes in the garden, and it's all ground into Noah's childhood.

I give it a shake and crumbs fall to the floor, because of course they do. Throughout Noah's elementary years, food particles collected in drifts under his seat, an endless snowfall of bits and pieces that never reached his mouth.

I fold the childhood as best as I can and slip it into the Ziploc bag. Then it's time to mop the crumbs off the floor and scrub the stickiness from my hands for the last time. The bag goes into a box under my bed, where there's another bag with Noah's babyhood in it, unopened since I shoved it out of sight along with the memories of blurry dark nights of grumpy cries and white, sour spit-up and mustardy blowouts staining the backs of overpriced infant clothes.

I decide to open the babyhood bag, just for a quick trip down memory lane. To my surprise, the reek of dirty diaper isn't as bad as I'd remembered. There's a hint of a different fragrance now, like milk-sweet breath from toothless gums. The babyhood has also grown softer, like a brand-new cotton infant blanket. As I rub my fingertips over it, I remember Noah's pudgy baby fist resting between my breasts, my hand supporting the folds of his bare back as we breathed in rhythm.

Like a fine wine, Noah's babyhood is changing with time.

One day, his childhood will also change, maybe into the smell of lollipop kisses and the watermelon shampoo that Noah doesn't use anymore. Until then, I shove the babyhood and childhood under my bed.

In the kitchen, I find the juice carton on the countertop. "Noah! Did you forget to put something away?"

He stumbles in, arms and legs so long and awkward. "Sorry, Mom." The juice goes in the fridge, and Noah pops a quick kiss on my cheek. "I'll remember next time."

I peck him back, spotting the constellation of red bumps on his cheeks and forehead. That didn't take long.

He's aging well.

IN THE CITY OF WARRING BABIES

Tara Campbell

When you moved here, we all tried to tell you it's not your fault—some babies just scream—and we know you've exhausted all possibilities because you've told us, exhausted, everything you've tried: every doctor's visit, all the cognitive tests and aromatherapy and audio therapy and teething rings and parent support groups and baby's first bloodwork and even your great-granny's poultice, just on a tiny patch, though, and only after testing it on yourself first, of course.

But nothing works: your baby won't stop screaming, and sometimes you almost feel like your baby's against you, like it hates you, and it won't stop wailing until it knows you're dead and buried.

Please know this is not at all true.

In this city, your baby's screeching has nothing to do with you. Your baby is at war with someone you don't even know: the baby down the street, or the one across town, or the one that was just born yesterday and is still in the hospital receiving its first instructions. All babies in this city are at war—which is not to say they are all warriors.

You might be tempted to assume that the most vocal babies, like yours, will be the fiercest—that they'll bring that brawling energy into whatever battles they face. You might also assume that not all of these battles will be literal, physical fights, because how many direct combat cultures are left in the world? Certainly not ours (on a good day).

So, you're perfectly right: The vast majority of the wars your baby will wage will be figurative. They may be individual battles (say, deciding whether or not to cheat on a test), or interpersonal (whether or not to let a friend cheat off of their test) or societal (whether to vote for candidate X or Y, or just run for office themselves and do all the cheating firsthand).

But your assumptions about modality are flawed. A riotous

baby might become a courageous fighter, or it might reveal itself as the one who cries "uncle" before the real fight has even begun. A quiet baby might grow to run and hide, or it might mature into someone who will wait and see, studying how to insert a stealthy knife, planning just when and where to strike for maximum effect. This knife might be figurative or literal, and you might be pleased or chagrined, depending. There's no way to know yet, and nothing to be done.

The baby at whom your baby is raging might be screeching back at this very moment. Or it might be cooing to itself in delighted mockery. Or it might be lying perfectly still, calculating serenely, the only sound in the nursery the gentle sucking on its thumb, perhaps the tinkle of a windup mobile rotoring plushies in circles above its crib, not that the baby would know, because it's likely gazing up at a point beyond the fuzzy yellow whales swimming their lazy rotations overhead, its eyes on a future coalescing in tune to your baby's screams, calmly choosing its weapons (money? knives? pride?), planning how to negotiate terms of engagement, and contemplating already how silently they will shatter, how smoothly the blade will slide through skin.

PART TWO:
teeth

SIMON

Naz Knudsen

Today, he toddles between the aisles, from fresh fruits to canned vegetables, from spaghetti to cereal. Everyone gushes about how cute he is. Everyone smiles. His mother tries to keep up with his excitement and the compliments. He insists on carrying a box of Cheerios half of his height. She helps him get it into the red cart before he reaches up to her and says, "Hold you?" Pulling him tight, she sneaks in little kisses on his curls and carries him on her hip. He loves the snuggles, but they won't contain him for long. As soon as those tiny new sneakers touch the ground, he tries to run, then tumbles and falls. In the middle of the aisle, he notices his reflection on the tile. He beams as tiny hands clap; there is a twinkle in those big, beautiful eyes. A shopper helps him up. She says he is so cute; she probably asks his name, too. Suddenly, he feels shy and hides behind his mom. His little head occasionally peeks at the strangers, those kind people who wave and smile.

Twelve years from now, he will meet his friends at his neighborhood park to play basketball. A lady walking her dog will call the cops to say there are people at the court who don't look like they live here.

Twenty years from now, the cops will pull him over at a traffic stop. The box of Cheerios sits still among the bags of groceries he has picked up on the way home. His mother, walking up and down the front porch, will call his phone with her long, trembling fingers, over, and over, and over again.

SUMMER FAIRYTALE

Laura Stanfill

O nce upon a time, so the story begins, three girls tuck their bare knees under their jackets, stuff loose hair into hoods, and wobble forward into the blackberries.

This neighborhood patch has taken over a house, wrapped its canes up and around like ribbons, sealed the door with thorns. Broken the windows.

The house looks out at us and raises its brambly eyebrows, as if to say, *What must I suffer next?* It has done everything it can to broadcast one message: LEAVE ME ALONE. And here are three girls, plunging into the thicket, yearning to make a sweet and private nest where adults can't reach them.

Perhaps the house understands this impulse.

I am the mother on the sidewalk, narrating what I'll tell the twins' mother when I return without them. "I let the children go," I'll say, as if speaking of a kite string or a waistline.

Perhaps I will bake bread and bring it as an apology to the twins' mother so I don't have to knock emptyhanded. Perhaps the other mother will pour honey over my offering and lick her fingers. Perhaps we will grieve over tea, dip our fingertips into the salt bowl.

And yet. My imagining of this moment does not deter the girls. Into the blackberries they plunge, still with their knees tucked safe, their hair under hoods. They look like fabric eggs, round and rent by giggles. They fit themselves one at a time through an opening. It's cool for summer. They can see a whole life in there, parentless. Eating sour fruit one drupelet at a time. Curling around each other like potato bugs when it rains. Losing wiggly teeth by biting on stalks. Spitting thorns like chicken bones into a designated corner. Braiding fallen twigs into hair ties and sleeping mats. They will make up their own rules. They will count bugs for math class. They won't have anyone to ask for one more episode, one more cookie, one more hour until bedtime, pleaaaase?

I wrote in my Cabbage Patch diary on July 1, 1987: *I've been too busy to write for a while because I've been with Gretchen. She is fun to be with and more daring than me. We found a blackberry tree and she grabbed a branch and started to eat.*

Poor sweet twins, gone forever, harvested by a hungry blackberry tree in the summer of 2019. My daughter will not accept such a fate. She'll materialize her pink camping knife and pare branches into filigree. "We are cold," she will say to the twins, "and thirsty, but look at the art that is possible!"

This particular blackberry patch has taken over not just a house, but a whole city lot. Two lots, the online map tells me— and surely devoured the property value—while local children wait for enough sun to trigger transformation. Every summer the thicket advances. These vines want to nourish the neighborhood. Before, I had to lift my firstborn so she could reach and pick. One bauble. And then one more. Not that one—it's not ripe—this one. Now unruly spills of fruit tumble around these girls' ankles. They don't need my strength or my permission. They can pick the puckery ones if they wish. They can pop handfuls into their mouths, grin purple at each other, know bounty.

An East Coast woman, new to this city, walks by and asks me what kind of berries they are. I wonder if she thinks we are studying a tree. Probably not. I believed in blackberry trees at age nine, and she must be in her thirties.

"My mother picked some yesterday, but they were sour," the woman admits. "This isn't the kind of city we know."

I called Gretchen *brave* in my diary because she helped herself to the wilderness. My parents wouldn't have wanted me to eat a bug or get my hands messy too far from a plumbed sink. Perhaps they warned me off all plants after finding me sucking on the hostas in our backyard, hungry for the clear, green spice of chlorophyll.

The twins and my daughter have discovered a dead end. They inch backward, thorns decorating their backs. I imagine their spines brazed to the canes, soldered, a ridgeline of triangles like tiny stegosauruses. But no—they scramble out, they are free. Not extinct. I help them pull a few thorns out of their jackets.

Now they readjust angles and find a clearer path, and I am no longer narrating, because I need to tell this newcomer the answer.

"Blackberries," I say. "And the sweetness is coming."

On some canes, with deep-hued berries dangling like earrings, it's already here.

I'LL BE SEEING YOU

Didi Wood

Dark but he's up, he's up, ears straining for the sound that woke him. Jason, crying out in his sleep, another nightmare? A car door slamming? The skitter of leaves on pavement?

No. Just the thud of blood in his own head, ragged breath through the desert of his mouth. Swallow. Breathe. There's nothing.

Wait. The snick of a switch—was that it? Yes: the kitchen light. Alex slips out of bed, glides to the top of the stairs. Listens. The refrigerator gasps open, jars juddering in the door.

She's back. She's in the kitchen. The yank and rattle of the cutlery drawer. Clink of knife on plate. His mother is here again, making sandwiches. She's humming something, slow and sweet, but he can't tell what it is.

His mother has been dead for seventeen years.

He doesn't want to go down, but he must. She's wearing the apron he made in first grade, a welter of handprints—his handprints—across the front in red paint, faded now with washing and age. He slides into a chair, and she smiles, still humming. What is that song? She smooths the perfect amount of Jif on a slice of Wonder Bread. He doesn't buy Wonder Bread—do they even make it anymore?—but that doesn't matter. He doesn't have grape jelly, either, but she's spreading some on another slice, again the perfect amount, shimmering like amethyst, just enough to moisten the sandwich but not so much that it will be too sweet or ooze out when he takes a bite. His mouth waters, and he swallows over the stone in his throat.

She made the best peanut butter and jelly sandwiches, he told his son, when Jason asked about the grandmother he'd never met. And she did. She does. Alex feels himself soften, swaddled in the glow of the kitchen, this pocket of peace in another dark night with his dead mother and her elusive tune and her perfect sandwich that he's starving for, he's starving, even knowing what comes next.

"Mom," he whispers.

She stops humming. She raises the knife.

Say: *I don't know what you want.*

Say: *I don't know what to do.*

Say: *Please go away.* Say: *I have a son.* Say: *I'm sorry.*

Say: *I wish*—what? What does he wish?

Maybe it doesn't matter. (It doesn't matter.)

Whatever he says, it's always the same. She slices the sandwich into triangles, first two and then four. The knife catches her thumb on the final cut, and after a breathless, suspended moment, blood seeps into the spongy white bread, saturating it, then spilling over the edge of the plate and flowing down the table toward him. He can't move.

"See what you made me do?" she wails.

"Dad?" Jason stands in the doorway, squinting against the light, his left cheek a constellation of sleep creases. What does he see? He clutches Chicky, stalwart bedtime companion and chief monster-fighter. "Dad, I dreamed you were a ghost."

Blood drips onto the floor, drip and splash and splatter, gathering into a puddle, a pool, a Rorschach demon with jagged, shrieking edges. It creeps toward his son's exposed toes. Alex can't move.

He can't move.

But he does, bursting from the chair so it slams to the ground. He turns Jason away, guiding him to the stairs.

Look back: no sandwich, no knife, no blood.

"What is it?" Jason yawns, wide, and Alex can see where the edges of his child's emerging front teeth slash through the gums.

"Nothing," he says. Glance back again. Make sure. "It's nothing."

WRITING PROMPTS: MARCH TO JUNE

Erin Fitzgerald

Describe a character's search for her keys and wallet one early spring evening, because her husband just called from school and told her to meet him in the emergency room. Do not mention why.

As the character from the first prompt drives to the hospital, recall one of the several times she's had to explain to non-Catholic Christians what the deal is with the Blessed Mother. Use this line of dialogue: "You don't *worship* her; you ask her to put in a good word for you when you need help."

Write a story that includes these words: *high school, auras, pediatrician, migraines, Advil.* Make it low-stakes when it actually isn't.

Create a teenaged character who, like most teenagers in stories, is quirky, funny, and smart. Make them old enough to understand what's happening to them. Make them wise before your first paragraph, because your story is about other ways that children grow up.

Develop a seemingly endless series of scenes in medical examination rooms, in which three characters are always the same and at least two others are usually different. In the first scene, give bad news from an emergency-room physician. Beginning with the second scene, which should be set in a neurosurgery exam room, have the news be very gradually better.

Have a character select a movie to watch while inside an MRI. Have the character select a movie they already know very well for the MRI after that one, because the machine roars too loudly to hear dialogue.

Consider the sentence "You must be going through hell right now," and how little pockets of hell hide in a red plastic basket full of Easter candy at Target, an infomercial at 3 a.m.

about rejuvenating middle-aged hair, in a green hoodie, and always inside the phone. Rename some of the contacts in the phone to: Someone At The Hospital, Check Voicemail In A Minute, and Pick This Up!!!

Find a reason to visit a children's hospital for a three-day stay. Notice the halls in the remodeled areas are curved, and the halls in the unremodeled areas are straight. Notice the posters on the bulletin boards in the elevators for upcoming *Star Wars* and superhero days. Notice signs of thoughtful curation in the gift shop. In the parking garage, notice a petite, elderly woman dressed in pale pink, wearing a white lab coat with HOSPITAL VOLUNTEER monogrammed in dark blue above the breast pocket. Notice that the front-desk volunteer in the Family Lounge identifies the numerous fish species in the Family Lounge fish tank for anyone who asks. Notice the large portrait of a yellow cheetah in the hall on the fourth floor that's made entirely from Lego pieces. Notice the cafeteria's jalapeño home fries because they are the best home fries you have ever eaten, and attention to craft brings the type of peace you have never re-sisted.

Imagine what it's like to be a person who respects the social-media blackout request, who texts ordinary or silly things at just the right times, who answers the questions from others that tire you to answer, who watches the live-action *Beauty and the Beast* movie in the Family Lounge, who sends unexpected treats from hundreds of miles away. Imagine what it's like to be a person who's read that article about rings of support in the *Los Angeles Times*.

Create a movie, book, play, or other work in the genre of gritty realism, in which the good guys don't ever stop what they're doing to share a message or a mission statement.

Describe all of the anesthesiologists you've ever met. Give one of them a large, shiny, red Craftsman toolbox on wheels. Make one a hipster with well-tailored, waxed, black jeans.

Write some dialogue between a mother and her teenager who's about to undergo surgery. Write about how the operating room looks more like a mechanic's garage than a TV medical-drama set. Write about the tube labeled *PROPOFOL* on the metal tray next to the teenager's head, and how it keeps making the mother think of Michael Jackson. Write what the mother and the teenager say to each other. Write about them laughing. Write about the mother seeing the teenager fall asleep before their eyes close. Write about the mother being escorted out of the operating room. Then, rip up those pages. The parts of the story that you don't share, aren't catharsis waiting to happen, they're magic that no one else has earned.

List all the things you would do in exchange for a shower and a decent nap. Meet other children and families in the ICU. Many have been there for a long time, and will be there after you are gone. Cross off everything on your list.

When you are in the Radiology waiting room for the fifth time, forget to bring your phone with you. Watch *Vampirina*, a cartoon about a family of vampires who lives in an otherwise-ordinary neighborhood, on the waiting room television. Later, write *Vampirina* fan fiction in which the neighbors, across their fences, quietly share their concerns over how Vampirina's family handles constant bloodlust.

Imagine what it's like to lose time. Everything happens that normally happens, like the mail shows up and the grass grows, but the rest of it—the weekend newspaper reading, the jokes about the cats' digestive adventures, the oil change, the laundry (other than four pairs of jeans that never got dry), the moving through!—doesn't happen. Imagine that gaining some of that time back takes much longer than it took to happen. Know that some of that time is lost for good.

Describe a brain tumor the size of an eyeball that was benign and is now carved up and incinerated, but lives on as a photo in your teenager's phone. Do this by stealing others' descriptions of its beige-blandness popping out from inside their skull, because you still haven't looked at that photo yourself, and maybe you never will.

Recall a time that there was so much in your world that did not belong to you, and that wasn't yours to share, but you need to say *something*. Wrestle with that need for a long, long time.

CROWN SHYNESS

Stephanie King

My wife is always looking for something that's missing. When our children were infants, she would steal away in the night to lurk over their cribs like the wraiths of legend. "But there's a monitor," I would say, and she would look up at me from the dark pools of her underslept eyes.

I didn't know her before. I wasn't on any of the search teams who swept through the woods behind the town park, futilely calling her first daughter's name. I only found out when I did a Google search on her after our second date, after what I thought was a Hallmark meet-cute, our hands bumping as we reached for the same zucchini at the farmers market. All the charm of small-town life I'd moved here to experience sucked out of me as I learned her before name, her before smile. Now I knew why she always moved with an air of sadness around her.

I know my wife still holds out hope while I, in the night, imagine her invisible daughter watching over our children's cribs, one after the other, keeping them safe. Surely such bad luck cannot strike twice. I imagine her taking their hands as they cross the treeline, guiding them through the forest as resolutely as Little Red Riding Hood followed the path. If she discovered a wolf in there, she will keep them safe from him.

They build their little fort in the woods, like all the town children do, the blankets and tarps and folding chairs of previous generations dotting the landscape, melting into the underbrush over time. They lie on their backs on their checkered picnic blanket and look up at the sky. She whispers to them how the treetops endeavor not to touch each other, shrinking away even as they sway in the same breeze. She shows them how cracks between the trees let the light in, for the smallest seedlings to grow, and for them to find their way home. Like the trees, their lives begin where she ends.

NEPHILIM

Meagan Lucas

You hang the streamers, though it hurts to stretch, because your husband cannot seem to do anything right, and has long since quit listening to directions. He sighs as you wince. A friend elbows him, shakes his head, "The sex is never the same," the friend says. You wish your problems were so simple.

Your jaw hurts from blowing up balloons. You're exhausted from cleaning, wrapping, and baking a cake in the shape of a number one, but everything is beautiful and perfect. You've hidden the knife, bleached the blood. (Neatness comes with experience.) Everyone sings. Everyone eats. They all praise the texture and flavor of your cake. "Mmm, buttery," some guy says. You grab a bite from an abandoned plate to see if you can taste it. The baby has mashed handfuls into her hair, but also into her mouth. You grit your teeth and ignore the hot throbbing beneath your clothes.

Your lips pull tight against your exposed teeth in the performance of joy as the other moms catch your eye and nod.

Years pass. Your child thrives. Friends and strangers praise how quickly you've bounced back from childbearing. In fairness, these first years were easy, you will realize later. You can still find some baby weight to lose under your spandex, and children will eat anything if it has icing and sprinkles. You watch their mouths as they chew. Occasionally, when they have crawled into your lap and told you that your tummy is a squishy pillow, you will gently squeeze their bodies: the back of an arm, the meat of a calf, and know that all the pain is worth it.

The teenage years are harder. Your body has become sleek and slim and stiff. Small. You are no longer a presence. There is bribing and bargaining. Plates scraped into the trash make you nauseous. They need you more than ever, but want you less. You worry you're not giving enough; they're not getting enough. But your husband is finally an ally. When he found you in the pantry with the knife the night before your baby's twelfth birthday, the blood drained from his face. You handed him the blade, turned your back, and pointed to your left buttock. He sighed because he loved your ass so much, the only piece of you that was still soft, but then he went to work.

When they finally move out of your house, when you think you might be able to build back some of your strength, some of your fire, that's when it's the worst. That's when you find yourself sneaking through windows to leave treats in their fridges, guilt-tripping dieting daughters and sons who should be watching their cholesterol. Atkins and paleo have made you change your methods. You drown in cooking shows, pore over *The Joy of Cooking*. You skip the cake and invite them to dinner, for chicken, healthy food. You are so small, a wisp of your former self. There is nearly nothing left. But they come.

Your daughter sits across from you, plump and glowing and brilliant and beautiful, perfection—and pokes at the meat with her fork. "Mom, this chicken thigh has the same birthmark as you. You know the one shaped like Kentucky on your stomach? Funny."

You press your palm to the still-raw spot where the mark used to be. You're hollow, only the suggestion of the woman you were, but she is bursting. You don't tell her what has nourished her all these years. You don't show her the scars. Instead, you watch her husband's hand on her thigh as she chews, and you know that she'll know soon enough.

SHAPED FOR FLIGHT

Kelle Schillaci Clarke

When Thea was small, she could slip through patio slats, slide under doorways, hide for hours beneath the teal loveseat until discovered by the cat, her dad and I still fighting over who had lost her. "She's a late developer," her pediatrician told us, holding a stethoscope over her body, splayed out flat across the exam table. "She'll develop her third dimension eventually," she said. "Try not to worry. Some children just take a little longer."

But Thea didn't seem to want to lose her flat edge. She used it in ways that made us not question her intelligence, which—developmentally speaking—seemed ahead of the game. She could spot a fight coming between her dad and me long before we even knew we were heading south. At the first sign of conflict, she'd lower her oatmeal spoon, slink from the barstool, and glide up the stairs like a stingray, her blankie trailing her like a poisonous tail.

"Is it our fault?" I asked her pediatrician at our next appointment, when I noticed other kids filling out.

"It's not *not* your fault," she said, deploying air-quotes as she tried to line up Thea's body against the height chart. Tall for her age, her flat head kept curving over, like those fortune-fish that curl up in the palm of your hand.

"We should find a new doctor," said Thea's dad on our way out, clutching Thea's flat hand, crumpling it like paper in his fist.

Sometimes, when I was done taking her to the park or baking cookies with her, on nonstick sheets as flat as she was, she'd roll herself into a tight scroll, wiggle a velour scrunchie around her middle, and I'd hand her off to her father like that, like a relay baton. "Please be careful with her," I'd say, worried he'd step on her, crease her, forget to latch her car seat, that she'd slide up and out the car window while he blasted the Grateful Dead.

I knew she'd round out eventually, find her form, like the doctor said. She wouldn't be anyone's doormat. And when she finally agreed to unflatten, we praised her growth. But she was unhappy. How would she protect herself from us now? So, I did what any good parent would do. Once thoroughly deflated myself, the arguments stopped, and I could wait for her under her bed while she was at school, cover her like a blanket when she cried out in the night. I could wrap around her, protect her. "Not forever," I whispered as she neared sleep. "Just for now. So you can grow."

And she did.

And with her slowly expanding width came a razor-sharp wit, cutting comebacks, and a swift flair for the dramatic, as if she were reborn as someone else. She wore only red, learned how to project her once-quiet voice. Now, instead of *me* arguing with her father, *she* did. With each exchange, her body transformed, muscles flourishing, fed by insatiable anger.

Then she turned on me, too.

"I don't need you anymore," she said, tossing me from her bed to the floor, where I seeped unrecognizably into carpet I no longer vacuumed. Eye-level with the purple shag, I could have blamed my tears on dust, but she knew she was breaking my heart when she said, "I don't need anyone," swung open her third-floor window, and pulled out the screen. She extended her still-thin arms, revealing a cluster of silver and red feathers underneath, juvenile wings jutting out, still soft and fuzzy at the base like baby hair.

"They're not ready yet!" I told her, but my words choked on dirt and dog fur, sank straight through the floorboards. Who was I to stop her, anyhow? Look what I'd become. I oozed my way between her and the open window, trying to trip her, change her mind, but she stepped over me with one foot, effortless, as if I were a puddle, then plunged the other into my gut. I wished I'd better prepared her—given her the tools she needed to fly. If only she'd stayed flat—her angles sharp, easily creased and shaped for flight—but she was no longer flat. We took even that away. I watched the dirtied soles of her bare feet lift into the window frame. She squatted for the briefest of moments, surveying the ground below, the sky above.

And then she was gone.

TOUGH TITTIES

Edie Meade

I am terrified to set you down, new baby I barely know by the name I gave you.

It was the coldest night of the year when you were born, but every night since has felt colder, and now we're both shivering wet from your constant spit-up, and I am sorry, and angry, and sorry for being angry.

I take you to the bathroom with me, hold you to my raw breast as I soak my wounds in a sitz bath. You cry yourself into a rigid arch, and I try not to drop you into the litterbox that's still sitting there, full of clumps beside the toilet, even though the cat ran away a week ago.

It's just you and me, new baby. We both have so much to learn. *The days are long, but the years are short*. Remember that. It's what you tell people whose turn it is to travel through hell. It's how the righteous say *tough titties*. They say it and then vanish so that we may suffer alone.

We must learn together, new baby. We learn by trial and error, trial by fire. This life is a trial of long-suffering days and tragically short years. My titties must toughen to this life.

For being so tiny, you are so very heavy. You are no heavier than the cat, Camille, whom I also named but called my baby. Camille, the cat who shared a life with me until I came home from the hospital with you, and then she bolted out the door into the bitter cold.

Camille would rather freeze to death—betrayed, unbaby-like—than to compete with you.

I used to call her my baby, but I'm not even sad she's gone. I'm too tired to look for her. I'm too tired to grieve for her. I'm too tired to feel ashamed that I do not grieve for her.

She is a cat. She is a cat. She is a cat.

I tell myself she is okay out there. Maybe she's peeking piti-lessly through the frosted bathroom window into our hell right now. Maybe she smells your spit-up. Maybe she smells my milk. My wounds. *Tough titties.*

Maybe she's safe and warm in a neighbor's house.

Maybe she killed herself on the road, and her body's frozen in a snowbank until I get out with you on a spring day and find her mummified ancient god-form and she lays a richly deserved curse upon me. Then I'll be forced to grieve for her because I will grieve for myself. Humans are selfish. That's an evolutionary advantage.

I think about Camille freezing to death with her agency and dignity intact, and I know she is stronger than me. I am not a cat. I'm afraid of the cold. I'm afraid of soft human skulls and limp human necks and infected human episiotomy stitches.

I'm afraid of you. Your tininess terrifies and terrorizes me. Please don't arch backward out of my arms and fall into a dirty, abandoned litterbox. Please don't rip my nipple off.

I am a bad mom, baby. I have few animal instincts. I was not born to be a mother, or even a pet owner. Sometimes I think I was not born to do anything but outlive cats. Our years are short, but theirs are shorter.

Camille is gone, and you are here instead. You beat her. It's just me and you, an arching baby who rips at my breasts. You won a battle you know nothing about, just as humans have always done in the animal kingdom. It's not really fair. You won a battle without having teeth, and now you're destroying me with those helpless, toothless gums.

You are so hard to hold, and I am so very tired, but the pain of your nursing keeps me awake. Thank you for that. I know it's your own pain that pulls you into an arch. That's a human trait, misery-spreading. You transmit pain through my every duct to a place somewhere near my heart, where fear of betrayal, fear of dropping you, fear of your fragility feels something like love.

That's a human trait, internalizing suffering, embracing pain. That's resilience. Or maybe empathy, another advantage we have over cats. We're in this together, baby. I will take the pain for you, because if I do not, you will end up broken in a litterbox.

BUMPS

Lydia Kim

I have large breasts, hypochondria, and a maternal history of mammary cancer, so I have been diligent. In the shower, I raise one arm, soap the cursed sac, massage the perimeter. The joke is, even a healthy breast is notoriously bumpy: sliced, it's like a cross-section of an orange, pulpy triangles pinned by a nipple. The self-exam is both recommended and pointless, performed, as it is, by an amateur.

I dreamed of bumps taking up residence in the exurbs of my body: marble-sized blips on the back of my neck, the crook of my thighs, the tops of my feet, of a single lump creeping along my fascia, propelled by peristaltic power, eventually expelling itself out a pore.

The children began as bumps.

I noticed a new bump in my armpit, another above my top rib. I went to the doctor.

"Not cancer," she said. "Just breast tissue."

Colonies of breast tissue. Scouts.

"Keep an eye on them," she said, making it my problem.

I poked at them, palpated them, the way one mindlessly wiggles a baby tooth. I stuck my hand down my shirt and worried them all day. I think this encouraged them, as if it were a kind of passive exercise.

I drew an outline around each one with a black marker, and they outgrew their boundaries, month after month. I considered the elective surgery to remove them but was ashamed. I'd waited too long. They were my problem now.

One day, during my perimeter massage, my finger slipped inside the armpit bump. It had a mouth, slippery gums. We startled each other. A tongue, lips. It cried. Instinctively I cupped it and shushed it. I felt a draft whoosh into my right rib and realized the other bump had a mouth, as well, and that it was also crying. I stood in the shower like a wet stone, two crying bumps, among the older, silent ones. I toweled off, held both my arms up and turned from side to side to look at the bumps in the mirror. Small, soft mouths with glossy gums, sitting at the peak of each bump. They hiccuped between wails until they stopped crying. I had to lower one arm to stroke the other bump. I had the feeling I imagine people have when they get a new dog: an immediate desire to take care of and be liked by tiny creatures.

Above the mouths, each bump had gentle divots where eyes might have been, and something dark pushed against dips. They looked fragile, cute. They looked like babies pressing their way face-first through a milky plastic.

It was easy to name them: Armie, for the armpit bump, and Eve for the other.

I had to sleep like someone falling backward in outer space, arms flung wide. That first night, they slept well.

I fed each mouth with a dropper, some warmed broth (I am allergic to dairy). They napped a great deal, emitting tiny snores, and smacked their lips when peckish. I boiled a whole young chicken for broth and ordered a set of droppers, ascending in size. I fed the bumps every two hours. I quit my job.

Motherhood meant so many things: I'd never be able to wear sleeveless tops. I'd have to walk like a bodybuilder to avoid smashing the children. I'd have to shop when they napped, lest they cried while I was out, posting a letter, pumping gas. I sent up a prayer of thanks that I did not sweat much, and never had body odor. I practiced telling prospective partners about their possible step-bumps. I understood that cats might hiss when I approached.

Like all children, they grew teeth, lost teeth, fought with each other and with me. Armie developed an allergy to chicken; Eve went through a phase where she only ate peanut butter, a mess. They pushed my buttons, wanted to stay up late. My trapezius muscles grew thick, strong. I dreamed of the children growing arms and grabbing at my nipples, reaching to stick things up my nose. They went through puberty, sprouting hair, then middle age, losing it.

We had almost ten good years.

The few hairs around their divots turned thin, then gray. Their lips chapped, they took less and less vegetable broth, their contours went to jelly. One day, they expired. No more wails from my dark places. I finally went for the surgery, cradled the Ziploc bag all the way home, placed them in the freezer. "My babies," I say, thumbing the frost from their lips.

SUGAR TIT

DeMisty D. Bellinger

What's stored in adipose tissues? Persistent organic pollutions, or POPs, as well as PCBs, PCDDs, PCDFs, and various toxic metals (such as lead and mercury).

Monisha was a little premature by Tatum's and my estimate. And they are a little small for a two-month-old child. But we love them just the same, and they seem to be growing into their placeholder name, even at that young age. Maybe they will identify as she and have a baby of their own one day.

In spite of what is in breastmilk, I am nursing them. We're sitting under the government-supplied UV-protected porch shield, basking in the safest rays of sun. I'm nearly asleep when Tatum nudges me lightly on my back with his big toe.

"Hey," he says, "I have a better idea."

Harmful chemicals now superseded the healthy fats and nutrients in mothers' milk. And not just human milk; of course, if it affects our milk production, why not cows, why not goats? "Breast Is Best" is now a dated and dangerous slogan, reserved for the impoverished and the so-called middleclass mothers who could not afford manufactured formula for offspring. For us, it's "Breast Is Good Enough."

Tatum holds a stuffed cloth made conical, similar to a pastry piping tube.

"Is that my old, stained shirt?" I turn slightly to him.

Unlatched, Monisha's eyes blink sleepily. Milk spills freely from their fat lips.

Feeding children tainted milk perpetuates the class divide; breastfed children are more susceptible to neural tube defects, stagnated or stunted growth, and other medical conditions, making them less able to compete in this hyper-capitalized economy.

"It's clean," he says.

"What is this?" I have my suspicions, but I want to hear him say it.

"We're survivors. I mean, our people been through some shit, right? Our female ancestors were forced into wet nursing—"

"Tatum! 'Breast Is Good Enough.'"

"No, it ain't, Daysha. We watch as the rich folks keep getting richer, their kids excelling in everything. Ours maintain the status quo or worse, get dumber."

"Don't say 'dumber.'"

"I mean, if our ancestors survived on this shit, which got us to where we are today, then it can get Monisha somewhere. I only want what's best for the baby."

I mull it over. I resist conceding. "Not all of them survived. And yes, I get it. I feel guilty every day," I say. "Bad enough to have had a baby nowadays, sure, and I do feel like I'm feeding them poison. Still, we can't give them a sugar tit; we know processed sugar ain't good for teeth and gums."

"It's not exactly a sugar tit."

"Then what's in it?"

He got down on his haunches and held out the bundle to me. Whatever is inside is tied in with hemp cord. "I did some research on all the nutrients growing babies need. Breast milk—healthy breast milk—has about seventy-five percent protein, water, fats, carbs, and vitamins. They need sodium, A, C, and D, calcium and iron. Some other things. So, I looked at foods that have these, like bananas and spinach, and I boiled them down, and yeah, I added sweetener, but it's added sugar-free. But baby, it's chemical-free, too."

I look away from Tatum and toward our child. Their lips are still open, forming an O shape, waiting for a nipple. Their tiny fist makes the sign for milk: pull, pull, pull.

"Just try it," Tatum says. I think about what it means to be a mother today, when there is an insurmountable wedge between wealth and poverty and between health and unhealthy. Even with working, even with our advanced degrees, Tatum and I would never be able to cross that divide, and if we continued to limit Monisha, neither would they.

"Give it here." I take the sugar tit from Tatum and give it to Monisha.

They are uncertain at first, but they take it in their mouth. Suckles. Their eyes close. The folds from Tatum's knot job look like flower petals. This appearance of flower, of growth, makes me think it's already working. They will thrive. Soon, they are asleep, their mouth slack and spilling a few drops of brown milk.

step·moth·er (step–muh *th*–er)

Melanie Figg

NOUN. 1. A woman who marries a man and expects—; A woman who has the nerve to— 2. One who raises another woman's child or children but is granted little authority with which to do so. 3. A woman met with resentment and suspicion; a threat. See: *target practice*. See: *homewrecker*. 4. A woman who is not a mother, and thus not natural. A freak of nature. An add-on; a woman who is said to steal another woman's children. See: *scapegoat*. 6. One who is often a target of relentless mayhem from the biological mother and/or a decoy for ammunition intended for the father. 7. A woman with an uncanny ability to become invisible at the dinner table after two hours in the kitchen, as well as at soccer games, band concerts, and most extended family activities. 8. A woman who prefers not to be the maid for small foreign tyrants. *Archaic:* a devious woman who enjoys baking, eating, or overworking small children; wicked.

VERB. 1. To perform any repetitive task and to be overlooked and/or to receive no credit for such, as in "She worked twelve hours straight, stepmothering thousands of plastic gizmos in the unventilated factory."

See also: *blended family*. 1. A family where one or both parents have children that are not related to the others, resulting in the physical and psychic experience of being put into a blender. Rhymes with: smother, why bother, oh brother, wept-mutter.

FEVER DREAM

Addie Tsai

There she was, my twin, my darling, or at least, that's what I used to call her in secret, in the shut closet of my room away from her. There she was, my twin sister in another hospital bed, but not in a hospital this time, but in a room where the bed floated, suspended in the air. She was dying. Her entire face was red as a rash, her body small as a child who doesn't make it long into the night. I'm not sure if it was a dream, or a fantasy. There were fantasies within the dream that made it so—I had a thought, and millions of hand-sized teddy bears appeared out of nowhere, in her two small closets, underneath her blankets, next to her ears—so many on the floor I fell to the ground. I had another dream, and made it so again—watched her hand as it reached for my cheek like applesauce. But it wasn't my cheek that was soft and pink like baby food, but her own. My little twin, my little darling of a duplicate, she was back in that bed again, although I hadn't recalled her leave, suddenly complaining of the way she had to limp on crutches the length of a stage to accept an award, her long-lost hip fastened together with a metal plate. But I have to tell the truth now. It smelled like rotten fruit in there, an untreated gash. And the teddy bears, they were real, but their ears had turned yellow, curling inward, like the neglected love letters of one who is rejected. And my sister, my darling little second edition, she was just an idea, a dream I left tied to the doorknob of my closet.

RINGLETS & KINKS

Marianne Worthington

The thicket in the chest when the phone pulses in the middle of the night. How the gut holds bad news; how the gut tangles, sickens, dies. The hospital, a maze, tortuous and meandering as the gut. The surgeon's curls, her face too young. Words she said to us—*total abdominal colectomy, intestines, ileostomy*—slithered and twisted above us like a serpent. A woman I don't know very well crying and praying loud over my daughter before surgery. The unsaid etiquette that stops me from slapping that woman off my daughter and dragging her out of the pre-op room by her hair. The sun turning up outside while we sit in a waiting room and look at our feet. The zigzag of pacing. Winding up a spiral staircase to the hospital giftshop. Who is this stranger saying my name and placing magazines and snacks in my lap? Stale coffee. TVs hawking junk. Arrows on signs steering us farther away from home.

In sleep, my daughter looks like my mother. In dreams, my sister becomes my daughter; my daughter becomes my sister. I call them by one another's names, and the plot line of the dream swerves as the dream decides who's playing the lead: my daughter my sister our mother myself. A long time ago: We take my mother to her neighborhood produce market to shop. My daughter is little, maybe four or five. At the market we see the owner, a man from the neighborhood my mother has known for half a century. He looks at my mother, at me, at my young daughter who is clutching my hand, says, "Well, I reckon you three come out of the same peapod." For so long I had not heard that kind of East Tennessee twang and verdict, the diction so easily assembled, wit as dry as a garden in drought. My heart dripped with homesickness.

The pain management team. The surgical team. The GI team. The minister from the Methodist church who visits and mercifully doesn't pray. Nurses cycling through the days. This ward is in a circular building. This ward is a grinding wheel that wears us down. How the ileum pulled through a hollow in the body looks like a rosebud, puckering, pink. "You have a pretty stoma," the nurse says. My father would have said, *Well, Little Bit got her a new shit hole*, and *did* say that to me in a dream after my daughter's surgery. I hear his voice when I sleep. He says my nickname, and I wake expecting to see him standing in the threshold. He laughs loud or sings out a gospel refrain or an old hillbilly boogie song by the Delmore Brothers in his high voice. (How I wish you could hear him talk and sing in my dreams.) My daughter's rosy ostomy resembles the Pink Parfait rosebushes clustering like flamingos around my grandmother's house, the outer petals opening and fading each spring, the center a resilient pink, coiled as if to protect the core.

WE, ROBOT

Maureen McEly

"I only invented the robot so I wouldn't—"

The mother broke off, remembering her audience, her children: a girl of six with Band-Aids on both knees, and a boy of three, eyes nearly hidden under bangs she needed to trim. Their small, curious faces stared up at her. She instantly rewrote the explanation in her head, deleting the dark days of loss, the wilderness in her mind she had barely escaped. She forced a smile and cut to the point.

"Anyway, it's here now, and it can do all the things I can't."

She maneuvered a large, homemade robot to the center of the room, its metal clattering like cans trailing after a car. Despite its ramshackle appearance, when she pressed a switch on its back, it lit up, eyes glowing a friendly shade of pink, an arm giving a jaunty—if jerky—wave.

The girl brightened instantly. "So, it can, like, run upstairs after us and play in the attic?"

"Yep."

The boy caught on. "Super-big swings? Cowapillar dance?"

The mother nodded.

Both children beamed. "And ride bikes all day and play tag and—"

The mother's smile tightened. "Everything, okay?"

Her children looked at each other in silent plotting, then, thrilled, at the robot, clearly already dreaming up a day of high-energy activities they'd been missing since she became ill. Seeing their transparent hunger for the things she couldn't do was a real knife in the ribs, which was unfair because this was her idea, not theirs. And it was going over exactly as she had hoped. Still, a fearful jealousy bloomed as they moved toward the back door.

"Wait."

They stopped obediently but didn't turn.

"Before you play with the robot, you have to always remember ..." *Don't say don't love it more than me. Don't say don't love it more than me.* "... to be careful." *There.*

But panic bubbled up again as she saw her eldest, her barnacle, the one who, still, at six, couldn't sleep without curling up beside her, eagerly take the robot's hand and walk again toward the door without a backward glance.

"... not to love it more than me!"

The girl turned at that, with the half smile she wore when emotions were confusing and too much, which made the mother feel bad, switching instantly into a singsong tone.

"Okay, have fun!"

The mother sat on the porch in front of the open back door, allowing the air conditioning from inside to keep her muscle weakness from worsening as it always did in the heat. Beyond, in the yard, her children played with their new companion, delighted. The robot could push them tirelessly on the swings. The robot could run. The robot was surprisingly (worryingly?) excellent at hide and seek. The day passed for the mother with the speed of a dental procedure, punctuated by the thrilled, out-of-breath laughter of her children. Hearing it from a distance made her ache.

Night finally fell, fireflies appearing one by one, the robot helping the children catch the bugs with a surprising gentleness. But after a moment, the girl turned and walked to the porch. She sat next to the mother on the steps. She was quiet.

"What's the matter?"

The girl was hesitant to reveal a problem with the biggest, shiniest toy she could imagine, but confessed: "The robot does not have any ideas. He only does what we say."

"Well, yeah, you have to tell him what to do."

"And he isn't silly. He doesn't do funny pig oinks or make up stories. He doesn't ever turn into a dragon when we least expect it." The girl looked up at the mother, sadly. "I thought he would be magic. But he's just, like, a toaster."

"Well, I'm very sorry about that," said the mother, hiding a smile as relief flooded her body like sunshine, like a drug.

The girl leaned against the mother's legs, her barnacle, curling up. "Can we snuggle while you tell me a story? The one about the clouds that ate the moon?"

"Of course."

The mother leaned in close to her daughter for a kiss on the cheek, but at the last moment oinked loudly instead, which made the girl collapse into surprised giggles. The mother wrapped her arms around the girl as they watched the darkening yard, where the robot lumbered over to the tiny boy with a handful of light.

Maybe this can work, she thought. *Maybe we can be happy.*

THE ONLY TRUE ESCAPE

JL Lycette

"Ten minutes," the replica says, "then time for Sheldon's nap."

Trixie lowers herself onto the chair, not wanting T1 to notice the pain in her gut intensifying. The last thing she needs is it reporting to Adem. She mutters under her breath as it exits the nursery, "Sometimes I wish Life-Aides, Inc., had given them more personality."

When Adem—her husband—had surprised her with the replica (she hates the word clone—after all, it isn't exactly *all* human tissue, what with the internal AI and all), she'd pretended to be happy. *Nothing but the best for you, Trix. So you can heal.*

But when it became clear that the physical damages were permanent (the doctors had told her it would be high-risk, but she'd insisted on a biological pregnancy; the pods had been so new at the time, after all), and the chronic pain, too, T2 had been added. Adem had given her everything. T1 for home, and T2 to continue her career.

The Life-Aides, Inc., jingle plays in her head: *Finally, you can have it all.*

But months had passed, and her pain never relented.

Sheldon falls asleep on her lap before the ten minutes. She tucks a silky lock of hair behind his ear. She's tempted to hold him for his entire nap like when he was an infant. But if she can get him in the crib, she might get a full hour to herself. If she calls T1, like she's supposed to, Sheldon might wake. Screw it, the pain's there all the time whether she lifts him or not. She grits her teeth and heaves him gently into the crib.

Success. She doubles over, hands on knees, not making a sound until the pain lessens enough to take a long breath. She gives in to the need to lie down herself. A nap will at least allow a brief reprieve from the pain. The pills only dull it—and her. Sleep is her only true escape.

She wakes sometime later to a hand on her shoulder and opens her eyes to her own face. Her eyes travel downward—her body in front of her, wearing business attire. She blinks. "T2? Why aren't you at the office?"

T2 disappears into the closet, reappearing with an armful of eveningwear. "Adem got tickets to that new production. The one everyone's talking about."

Trixie rubs her eyes and sits up. "I guess I should get ready then. But isn't this more of T1's job?"

T2 tosses aside a sequined top. "Your programming's amazing."

"Programming?" Trixie laughs but then stops. Something in T2's eyes makes her scramble backward.

T2 crosses its arms. "You actually think you're me."

Trixie gapes at it. "I'm—"

T2 spouts a string of numbers.

Something shifts in Trixie's brain. She glances down, taking in the bed. What is she doing here? She should be at work—

"Sorry to do that to you, T2," the other Trixie says. "I know it's disorienting."

Trixie shakes her head. "It's—I'm not—"

"It should be coming back to you now."

Trixie's memories shuffle, blur. She's a Life Aide, Inc., replica. No—that's crazy—she's Sheldon's mother. No, she's T2. *No.* She's *Trixie*, and T2 must be malfunctioning—

Her pain. Her pain is gone. The pain the doctors told her was the cost of motherhood.

But none of it has been real.

"W—why?"

The other Trixie dons a statement necklace and admires herself in the mirror. "Because Adem doesn't understand. I don't want to be only Sheldon's little mommy." She affects a yawn. "Booooorrrrring."

"But, the pain—"

The look the other Trixie gives her contains a measure of sympathy. "With previous models, it didn't work without the pain."

A twinge of alarm passes through Trixie. "Sheldon—"

"Relax. T1 has him."

Something clicks inside Trixie's head. She knows who she is and what she has to do. She points to a snag in the other Trixie's tights. "You'd better change those."

The other Trixie glances down. "Damn it."

Trixie follows her into the closet. She shuts the door behind them and reaches for a belt.

Five minutes later, she exits the bedroom, her sequin top sparkling, and follows the sound of voices to the living room. Without the pain, she feels so light, so free. Almost giddy. She takes Adem's arm and exchanges a look of understanding with T1.

"There's a slight mess in the closet. Take care of it before we get back, please."

INSOMNIA

Jo Saleska Lange

The dark figure at the edge of your bed is your son, who has begun sleepwalking in the months since his mother died. You hear him at night: his bedroom door yawning open, tiny bare feet pittering across wooden floors, drawers groaning, books hitting the floor. They say he's fine, that he'll grow out of it eventually. You roll into your pillow, which, after all these months, still smells like fresh bread and lavender.

But you feel your son's unseeing eyes on the back of your neck like cold fingers, hear his saliva catch with every exhale. You know sleep will never come, anyway. You peel off your blanket and go to him, ever-so-gently cup your hands over his fragile shoulders and guide him down the dark hall.

When you reach his bedroom door, he startles. Sharp inhale. A swimmer coming up for air. He grabs your hand—beartrap-strong grip for such a little one—and looks up at you with eyes that cut through the darkness like moons. "I'm frightened," he says. Not scared, not nervous, but *frightened*. He has always echoed his mother. He lowers his voice to a whisper: "There's someone under my bed."

And you recognize this ploy—oh, yes—you played it a hundred times with your dad, so of course you play along: "All right, bud. I'll take care of it." You lower yourself to the ground beside his bed, summon your most menacing voice: "Whoever's there, you better skedaddle." And then for extra effect, you reach deep under the bed to prove it's all clear.

Only, you do feel something. A warm body tenses at the end of your fingertips, and you laugh a little because you know it's just your cat, Miss Scarlet. But when you turn to tell your son "all clear," you see that he is holding Miss Scarlet, stroking her tail, cooing the same honeyed lie your wife told until the very end: "You're okay, you're okay, you're okay."

PIEZO

Mandira Pattnaik

Failed. Failed again. Failed a third time. Between lavender-colored walls of the clinic and an eggshell home, I've agonized over these words. Just as I have over the Greek word for push: *piezo*.

Ever since they told me piezoelectric effect works in a handheld ultrasound transducer.

I've hated these trips, even though I've always suspected Houdini in my belly. Every time they've ended in another failure, I knew of the success over which I had no control.

This dewy morning, you're driving me. Sweat beads on your forehead, unshaven face. I love how your jaw stays firm. When you tuck me in, and the engine thrums, Houdini prances and whispers, laughs and sings. He crawls against my skin, caresses with his knee upon my navel.

Outside, I find the world is born anew, a spectacular light-burst, erupted like seedling on barren land.

At the bends where the dirt road meets the highway, you ask, "You, okay?"

I nod, return to remembrances of revolts within, spasms of doubt, hope, doubt. How blank days yelled at me, how I slashed dates off the calendar, waited for another IVF cycle to begin. "Will it ever end?" I'd beg a reply. You didn't answer—stayed put a six-hour flight away, concealing your pain, patrolling borders in a stiff olive uniform.

I unleashed the conjuration.

The tires screech, a puddle where you apply brakes, glance at me, apologize. I laugh. You laugh, too. Squeeze my hand—it's the same word, *piezo*. Instead of shuddering, I revel, squeeze your hand back, feel the warmth. How I missed it when you avoided coming home, even for holidays. I understood, prayed I vanished without a trace.

You're a mere prop in the show today, a high chair on stage, or confetti shower when the magic happens.

Rolling the window down to let in envelopes of winter or mist, I swallow the all-bestowing air like blessing. There! On the cleavage of clouds, a rainbow, a moment's miracle. On a morning like this, after you had said we should quit, we'd talked. About magical chances, hope in a billion frigid galaxies. I'd only cried, imagined holding candles in eternal darkness, convinced you. We watched Adrien Brody as Houdini that afternoon on TV. Let "Bullet Catch for the Kaiser" play as we made love.

At the parking lot, you lean to my side, whisper, "I love you." Break the spell of some ancient ache. My body feels heavy and hungry. Breasts, full with sweetened nourishment, hurting. You hold me, precious and rare, as we walk inside; attendants ease me gently on the examination table, pearl in my oyster.

The piezoelectric effect begins to generate signals to the stress applied on my huge belly. Images flitter on the grainy USG screen. I see Houdini's tiny fists, breaking the shackles, pumping at us to rejoice a trick he's accomplished.

We're the awed audience applauding: Houdini emerging from a beached whale's belly.

(again)

Miriam Gershow

Jacob called for Irene, same as every night, Reenie waking to a clot in her throat, her head barely fuzzed with dreams, her limbs lithe and ready. A body learned, even in sleep.

She held herself in Jacob's doorway, the sound beneath his bed wet and squelching. The boy whimpered.

"Pull your feet under the blankets," Reenie told him, forcing her voice. She could be talking of cucumbers or coloring books. He was tiny in his bed, made tinier from the noise and the sulfurous smell, which would give way to sweet rot, a smell like no other but the closest: the compost out back as she turned it.

His room blazed, nightlights in every socket, a projector of stars on the ceiling. For a while, she'd kept his light on, Jacob lying taut and alert, eyes wide, an old man by morning. He had to sleep. It was like keeping him fed and sheltered, making sure the albuterol was in his bag, the EpiPen. "Sorry to report," the vice principal always began the calls: Girl plus errant granola bar. School nurse plus latex Band-Aid. Bumblebee. Jacob's eyes would be dark with bags at pickup, his face pale. The way Jacob smiled when he saw Reenie broke her all the way open, such a goddamn good kid, even when also a ghost.

"Mama," he said now, barely.

"I'll come in." It got worse if she went in, and yet. "But only this far," she announced of the recliner, a bargain.

This, the same recliner where she'd once nursed him, the faintest hint of milk in the fabric, or maybe that was only wishful thinking. The noises from beneath the bed redoubled: a fat and sopping bud breaking through marsh—no, a deformed calf breeching. From the recliner, this was all Reenie could do, try to name it. The scaly hand snaked up the side of his mattress to grasp his ankle, the crackled yellow nails swimming back from Reenie's childhood. She could feel the hurt in her own ankle like a memory, but a memory with nerve endings.

The one night she could not take his crying (more than one), she'd snapped: "Stop it!" ("Shut up!"), and Jacob had forced himself to lie quiet, though his body shook, a little at first and then uncontrollably, eyes glistening in the half-light, and she'd promised herself, never again (again). She lay in his bed as penance, coiling herself, the worst thing she could do, the scaly arms barely abrading her skin before grasping Jacob harder, tighter, making him gasp. Oh, how he clung to her. In the morning, she twisted her head in the mirror to see the ten snaking trails along her back—spots of broken skin, dried blood. When he was a baby, his fingernails had been soft like paper. She'd been fascinated by this, stunned. No one had told her about the fingernails. She bent them forward, one by one, under the force of her own fingers.

Jacob's crying grew more ragged, though he tried to swallow it, and she knew his face was red from the effort. She knew without looking, easier not to look.

"See if you can," Reenie said, "be still." This is what she'd done as a girl. It did not help. Nothing helped, which Jacob already knew, even if he tried to trust her into unknowing. When she very slowly leaned from the chair and stretched her arm to him, he very slowly gripped her hand, though once he had it, dug in. She would come away with red sliver-moons in the fleshy pad of her palm.

She'd trimmed his baby nails by biting them—the pediatrician told her to, the first advice she'd loved, his body pale and perfect and unbearably hers. There was so much she'd known to be unprepared for: sleeplessness, chapped nipples, piss and shit and piss and shit and piss. But no one had unprepared her for the impossible tenderness or the pain of an overfull heart. She'd torn at his fingernails with her teeth, stopping herself from fingertips, dimpled knuckles, fat arms, though she swallowed the bits of his keratin quick, letting them scrape and tickle the back of her throat, knowing even then, so near to the beginning, the rare gift of hungry beast fed.

ADAPTATION

Pip Robertson

The feral cats are thriving, so the bird people set traps. Ana volunteers to check ours before school. It should be a quick job—five traps on the forest track at the back of the house. But it takes longer and longer each morning.

"What are you doing out there?" I ask.

"Nothing," she says, pushing breakfast around her plate, smiling to herself.

So, one morning I follow her pink jacket through the trees. She jogs the track, checking each trap. At the fifth one, she stops, bends down. If we catch a cat, we're meant to call the bird people, who will deal with it humanely.

But Ana does something with the trap, then there's crashing through the undergrowth, and a shriek that makes my stomach lurch.

I wait.

Ana runs back down the path, wiping her mouth. In the moment before she knows I'm there, I have never seen her look more alive.

There was a biting phase at kindergarten. She'd said sorry over and over to the boy with bruises at his throat. Then, chasing games that got out of hand at school. The principal said Ana just had energy to burn, and sent her for a run at lunchtime, rain or shine. That seemed to solve it, and I had thought we were in the clear.

I lock the door and keep the key around my neck at night. But Ana won't even look at the forest. She closes the curtains, won't take the shortcut.

After school, she does her homework in the visitor center while I tell tourists how moa lived here once—a bird taller than a man on another man's shoulders. I tell them about the flightless night parrots, and the pigeons as big as chickens. The only native mammal is a bat smaller than your finger. When people arrived with our hungry new animals, the birds didn't stand a chance. They'd never anticipated beasts with teeth.

We walk home together. Ana keeps her head down, eyes averted from the trees.

Her father was a German backpacker. He'd been in the visitor center, pushing the buttons that fill the room with the recordings of long-dead birds. He had nowhere to stay, so I said he could crash with me. I never got a last name.

Ana knows this, but sometimes I say I picked her off a tree, or fished her out of a puddle after rain. Sometimes I say I found an egg in an abandoned nest and wrapped it against my body to keep it warm.

"Then, one night I woke to tapping next to my skin. It got stronger and stronger until I felt it in every bone."

"Were you scared?"

"Of course. Then, a crack appeared. I looked inside—"

"What was there?"

Sometimes I say a monster. Most times I say, "You."

The days shorten. Ana has no appetite, no matter what I cook. Saying goodnight, I linger in her room. I talk about holidays we could take, offer to drive her into the city to buy new winter clothes. I say we could paint her bedroom, any color she chooses.

"If you like," she says, to all of my suggestions, and curls up away from me.

When I look in later, her legs are twitching, running in her dreams.

We are almost through winter when the principal asks to speak to me. Ana waits in the playground. He tells me she has been snarling at her classmates.

"Snarling?"

He bares his teeth to demonstrate. We watch her, bounding the wrong way up the slide, leaping to the ground. She's always been small for her age, but strong.

"I'm trying," I say.

Ana crouches, wraps her arms around her legs, and rests her head against her knees.

"You know," he said, "it's easier to work with a child's nature than against it."

I knock on her door. "Ana, time to go."

She's ready.

It's cold. Our breath is visible as we walk along the track.

"The mornings are getting lighter," I say, but her mind is already elsewhere. We stop. "Remember—" I start, but she interrupts.

"I know, I know, nothing with feathers." She drops to all fours, waits for my signal.

I give it, and she's off, into the forest, to catch her fill.

MILQUETOAST

Amy Cipolla Barnes

I pull my children from a starter sourdough ball. It's over one hundred years old and lives in my refrigerator next to the mustard and moldy cheese: the family starter. I grab yeasty bits of baby in the jar marked *B* to knead the baby until he is the right size and texture.

There's a Bakelite handle on my stomach and a smudged glass door.

"I have a bun in the oven." I point at my belly.

My husband sighs at the pun.

He feeds me flour every day. It's what I crave. It's what the baby craves. A new starter bubbles up in my mouth, and I set the timer. Fifteen minutes. We count together to a *positive*.

My mother's face appears in my morning toast. I try to scrape her off with a butter knife. Her burnt black hair falls off into the sink, and then her eyes follow. She lives in my toaster because I won't let her live in my house. I hear her at night rustling, ready to impress her impressive face on Pop-Tarts and toasted toast.

I read that Queen Elizabeth is older than sliced bread. I wonder how she ate her bread when she was pregnant. With butter? In giant hunks that a lady-in-waiting ripped off for her before it was pre-sliced? Did she slice off her three children with a royal sword, coating them with sticky marmalade so they couldn't escape her side? It explains a lot at midnight when I contemplate how she must have scraped off Prince Charles' hair from his toast portrait. And also William's. *Scrape. Scrape.* With a British accent and a sterling-silver tea knife.

The doctor uses a serrated bread knife to slice me open when it's time. He saws away until he can pull out a tiny bread loaf. A silent one. Bread doesn't cry. I know that. But I want it to cry. I want to hear it wailing through the air holes in the structure of the gluten, the structure I built in my mason-jar belly full of yeasty starter.

I want to see Jesus in my toast. I want to see the Virgin Mary on my tortillas. It would be easier to explain to the nurses and the doctors and my husband. Instead, I dig deep into the starter and find just enough for another child.

My mother's face is again disapproving on the toast. I wash black bits of her face down the sink and toss the bread heels to the birds.

LOSING BUNNY

Melissa Saggerer

The day Melissa lost Bunny we were visiting Grandma, her tiny apartment overlooking the harbor. The biggest fish I've ever seen was hauled up, an Atlantic Bluefin Tuna. It felt bigger than the whole diner where we'd just eaten, its rubbery blue-black skin only a few feet from us, too fresh to smell, crane movements deafening as it swung closer, dripping. We lined up at the water's edge like thirsty animals. Melissa's jaw dropped, saying, "*This* is what fishermen do?" Maybe that's when she dropped Bunny, with her jaw.

Bunny was a small muslin creature made with love, stuffed with it, squeezed into the cotton, the kind that never left Melissa's fist for long. The kind she couldn't sleep without, sending us searching through damp grass with flashlights.

We looked under the piano, looked over Grandma's Oriental rug, littered with pink flowers. Every dark corner was illuminated, searched. We retraced our steps, past the flat flanks of the leviathan. We revisited the diner, looking for signs of floppy ears, hints of his browning, loved-up seams.

I piled bereft Melissa and her older brother into the car without Bunny. "Don't worry, we'll get you another," I said, calm as I could, fastening her little toddler seatbelt, wondering if words were enough to shield her from tears, a trip without her amulet.

At home, she waited patiently, without pulling skirts, as I cut cloth, embroidered features, fashioned a little checked apron.

Old Bunny and new Bunny were so similar, siblings, twins, shadow-selves. The space between new and old closed quickly, clutched in her hot hands, tighter than ever, more vigilantly galvanizing love now that she knew loss.

Days stretched into dreams into birthdays into school days, and eventually, Bunny stayed on pillows more than he was carried. Was cradled at night, not daily portaged.

Melissa came to love the story *The Velveteen Rabbit*. She wanted to believe it so badly. She left Bunny with his dust cousins under her bed, hoping if she forgot him long enough, he would become real.

He's in her dresser drawer now, still waiting to transform, creaky knees, a dirty silver—stuffing blooming out of his chest. Maybe she needs to switch her hope now to old Bunny, so intertwined with her forever friend that it feels a betrayal to acknowledge there was a time he had a different face. Maybe *old Bunny* became real. He was truly forgotten, not just a game. Maybe he took one look at that tuna, its fate in this cruel world, and fled for the hills.

CLEAN BOYS FOR HEAVEN

Frankie McMillan

O ur mothers make the hot water, but our fathers give us the bath. Once a week, us boys fight to be near the taps, fight to get the soap, lathering our hair into spikes, eyes squeezed shut, all hard knees, sharp elbows and brave chests, our hearts plumbing just below the surface. Our fathers wash behind our ears. They wash under our arms, between the fingers and toes, between the legs, flannel our backs, and scrub our knees.

"Warshin' makes clean bodies, clean minds," they say. They sit on the side of the bath, arms all soapy, and say, "Ask me anything you like."

"Can a man walk on water?" we say.

"You boys been fooling down the lake?"

We wring out the flannels, watch the water pour down over our knees.

"Only Jesus can walk on water. Anybody else tell you that is a false Christ."

We don't ask any more questions. We don't ask why Big Joe tried to walk on water and come out naked and spitting mud, nor do we ask why anything that goes in the lake comes out sick. They want us to ask different sorts of questions, like: When is the rocket ship taking us to heaven? Will there be lions lying down with lambs? Will we be fathers one day, just like them, and have quiversful of children all laughing their heads off at the wonder of it all.

We stand in the bath to show off our arm muscles. Our fathers push on our arms, and we push right back. They line us up to see who's the tallest. Then they carry us, wrapped in towels, to the fire. We far too big to be carried, we know it. We stand by the fire turning our bodies round and round. Our fathers sit on the sofas, roll cigarettes on their arms, look proudly at us.

When they weep, when they ball their fists to their temples, we don't ask what's wrong. We already know what's wrong. They're missing us before we gone.

At the meeting, some fathers say, "We'll never get this runway made," and "What about the older boys following behind the tractor with wet sacks?" but the elders say, "No tractor. Even with the wet sacks, there's too much fire risk."

So, how come some nights the tractor is cranked up? How come the long-haired man on the tractor is chugging around in circles, one hand holding a lamp over the steering wheel, light bouncing over the paddock, other hand working the gears? How come he takes the old Ferguson at full throttle on the bends without a roll?

We never stay awake long enough to see how the man stops the tractor. If he kills the tractor with the choke. Or if he uses the belt-drum brake. Or whether he doesn't have to worry about things like flooding the engine but just soars clean out of his tractor seat, his saintly legs kicking the air as he rises.

The dogs start barking way before we see the billowing dust. Our fathers put down their scythes, wipe their grass-stained faces.

The Rawleigh van lurches up the long drive and stops by the big runway. The man jumps out, shakes the hands of the fathers. His eyes flicker over the cleared patch of earth, and up to the new signal tower. Our fathers fold their burned arms and wait. Us kids wait, lying flat on our bellies in the long, feathery grass.

"Are you expectin' an aeroplane?" the Rawleigh man says. He rubs his pale hands, says the back of his van is full of goods, canned goods and farm goods, medicines and ointments. He laughs. "It's free to look," he says.

Us kids inch closer, but not so close he could reach out and snatch us.

The Rawleigh man says we talk like Americans. "Are you hillbillies?" he says.

He gives us each an aniseed ball to suck, while keeping an eye on our fathers. They run their big, callused hands over the gumboots.

"These will last you forever," the Rawleigh says.

When they don't answer, he waves toward the kitchen, tries calling our mamas over. He holds up a round tin of ointment, patterned with blue and gold. It flashes in the sun.

"For all your little aches and pains," he cries.

Us kids start laughing like Americans.

The Rawleigh man packs up the back of the van again.

Our fathers don't want the forever gumboots. "Not suitable," they say.

We watch the van drive away, gettin' smaller and smaller, sun glinting on the rooftop.

THE EAVES

Audrey Burges

H e says we should move because you'll keep returning, over and over, only to be lost again. It has happened already, three times. He points toward the cobwebs in the corner, the wooden beams I thought held character before he said they held you, meaning those lengths of wood have a privilege my arms have never been afforded. My arms would be better at it than my belly, I promise.

It will happen again, he says, and I can't tell him I am counting on it. I will keep counting. It's the only thing that counts anymore: that you are here and will be again.

Each time you leave us, you return to this house that has always and never been yours. You have clawed a perch into this place, watching us from the eaves. You are looking for a vessel to the waking world but keep picking the wrong one. My hull is not sound and cannot bring you to a safe harbor.

I don't know how he got this idea about where you go and why you come back, this repeated reincarnation, if reincarnation kept skipping over the part where you actually draw breath and live. He found some old story about lost infants and the places they haunt, the ways they find to rejoin the living for some short time, a changeling in the womb. But they can't stay, and they get pulled away into the realm beyond this one, over and over. That is what is happening, he thinks, and so he wants to leave. He spends the small hours of the morning scrolling for any explanation. I suppose the myths and fables he finds are better than science, better than support groups and FAQs and pinning the blame where it should go.

This is the story that sticks with him—this round-eyed owlish vision peering from the rafters, waiting for a chance. It's the reason he decides you're not sticking with us.

Not sticking with me. Not sticking in me. I am slick and slippery inside, a smooth void where you can't find purchase. I dig my fingers into the folds of my stomach as if I can model an appropriate grip for you. "Like this," I whisper. "Really dig in."

I hope you watch the way my fingers leave bruises, a lighter blue than the ones from the shots, but sharper. Each time I sit on the threadbare upholstery and lean my head against the wing of the chair, where the pressure has worn the chintz flowers away, I hope you're there in that dark corner, the one with shadows no lamp can banish. I take shallow breaths that do not reach my abdomen, my hands gripped like a vise around the tender parts you left behind. *Use your teeth, baby. Use your nails.*

I sit beneath the beams of this house he wants to leave, but I will not leave you here alone. Three times, four, as many as it takes. I sit beneath the ceiling that is the floor of the room where I have not laid you in your crib, where I have not rocked you in the padded glider, where I have not pressed my lips against each of your small toes and whorled fingertips and felt for sharpness there, that unexpected razor's edge against your smooth newness.

I have the tiny clippers in a drawer, waiting.

But if I can ever get you down from the shadowy peaks of this house and into my arms, if I can ever get you to stay, I promise I will never cut your nails. I will bite them, gentle as a whisper, with my teeth.

I will swallow them, those little crescent moons of you, and keep them in my belly. I will bank them away like seeds against harsh seasons. I will store them for the next time you slip away.

THE DEAD JAR

Michaella Thornton

I f I am Demeter and she is Persephone, she is safe now and it is spring. She is life and a cool breeze; I am death and fertile decay. Snake-haired and wild, I am a mother who will scour the earth for her lost daughter and create droughts from the floods of my grief.

Foam blocks the size and color of paving stones suck my feet and legs down deeper and deeper into this disease-breeding chasm. This was my bright idea, to show my four-year-old daughter that her middle-aged mother wasn't as old as she thought. That I still had life in me yet.

There are duct-taped bars to grab hold of, just out of my reach, pedestals from which to jump. There is a beacon of fiery light just to the right of me, letters that spell out the heavenly word "EXIT," but my panicked redistribution of weight finds me drowning in plain sight in this fuckery of foam blocks, family, filth, and fun.

Before my swan dive, before I hoist my bleating child to safety, I don't ask myself: *Why are no other parents in this foam pit? Why don't I balk at signing this lengthy liability waiver? What about the litany of broken necks and legs, spinal cord injuries, paralysis, the alarming cases detailed on personal-injury lawyer websites, the American Academy of Pediatrics' somber warning about trampoline parks?*

Without a lever to pry my rubenesque, forty-something body up and over the lip of the pit, my young child watches me with scientific detachment, the same way she views the bugs we scavenge for her "dead jar." The old mustard jar with a dented forest-green lid contains bugs she has collected from the garden, the park, the window ledge. Her burial jar holds an innocent white moth, a fly, an ant, a black-and-yellow garden spider, a honeybee with saffron-colored flecks of pollen on its belly.

Some find my daughter's fascination with dead bugs macabre; I find it charming. I want to study life and death with her. I want to ensure, as Mary Oliver wrote, that she doesn't just visit this world.

Meanwhile, I remind myself to breathe as she studies me, sitting with her coltish legs pulled up to her chin, as I try not to hyperventilate. For a few sacred minutes, my anxious mind dives below the surface, into a lost sea of errant grippy socks, friendship bracelets, lost teeth, lip gloss flavored like sugary treats and soda pop, chewed gum, pocket-sized erasers in the shape of dinosaurs and tacos and dolphins.

Will this memory scar my daughter, mark the exact moment when she realizes her mother is:

    a.) Vulnerable

    b.) Out of shape

    c.) Going to die someday

    d.) Brave

    e.) Stubborn

    f.) All of the above?

From the sidelines, the Greek chorus of parents watches me, wondering if I will make it, like the mosquito my daughter traps one evening before bed. When I tell her the insect will be dead come morning, she singsongs, "Okay!" like a gleeful siren, like a foregone conclusion, like a young Emily Dickinson writing love poems for death.

When I wake the following morning, the large mosquito is still alive, hovering a centimeter or three, invariably collapsing, onto the dead bodies below it. There cannot be much air left.

I feel pain and regret, even for this bloodsucker. How much longer can it fly? I don't like mosquitos, but there is recognition in seeing something in agonizing mid-escape, like when I finally push my legs off of a padded pillar and winch my way up and over the ledge of the foam pit with my daughter's merciful hand extended.

She laughs in her sleep as I open the back door and unscrew the lid.

THE PLAYGROUND DADS' COVEN

Masha Kisel

No, we don't use magic spells! We just call ourselves a coven when we need a laugh. But each of us dads at Orchardly playground in Oakwood, Ohio, does possess a special power. Your kid gets scraped up? Andy's the healer. He was an EMT before he became a dad and always carries his first-aid kit, a real wizard with the Band-Aids and dry ice.

Tom's the snack dad—he has a trunk full of cheese crackers and grime gummies. Sometimes he'll share his latest baking project. "Try my gasoline-soaked cupcakes," he blushes. Always unsure of himself since that bake-sale fire.

I am the one with the voice—the artist in the group. I never brag about my former life, how far I'd made it in *The Loud Yell* competition. But that was *before*. Now I use my hidden talent to call the kids home for dinner.

While the wives are at work, we commiserate, feeling a bit guilty about our tiny betrayals. But once the game begins, we can't stop one-upping each other.

"Deb once wore mismatched holsters to the board meeting," Tom giggles. "I suppose I was partially to blame. I made decaf by accident that morning!"

"Well, Jeanine bought herself a red Jag for her fortieth-fortieth, and the first night she takes her friends out to the tunnels, her Jag gets towed! She was pissed!"

"In more ways than one!" Andy flashes his perfect jade veneers. His wife's a dentist, so he gets his cosmetic upgrades for free.

"Sometimes during sex, Antonia calls me by my brother's name," Toby drones in his deep bass. "Jim's a colonel in the Cloud Force."

We all get quiet, then explode with laughter.

When the kids are busy in the magnetic fields playing "Whose Laser Eye?" we can step out of our dad roles and just be ourselves.

I'm not complaining. I knew what I'd signed up for when I decided to become a father. You can't have it all. I can still practice my screaming in the shower. And isn't the daily beauty of fatherhood enough? I play Russian roulette with the kids, I bleed into vintage ceramic vases, I take our rottweiler/pug mix to his piano lessons, beaming with pride to watch the clickety-clack of his paws progress from scales to Scriabin. But sometimes ...

"Do you ever wish we were real warlocks?" I ask my playground dads. The kids are all taped shut after a day of heavy artillery, and we swig pinesap on my sex swing. "What magic feats would you perform?"

"A bit of appreciation," Andy sighs. "Would that require a supernatural act of sorcery?"

"I'd transform into a bouquet of roses. So my wife would finally sniff my petals, reciprocate for once," complains Tom.

And what would I wish for?

I'd give myself a set of lungs that make sound travel. I'd scream and scream until my wife, Sharon, who refuses to pick up her telepathy signal while she's at work, hears me and comes home on time, before the cryptodon roast gets cold.

PART THREE :
cages

A GOLDEN WARNING

Mike McClelland

One of my quarantine distractions was playing the recent remake of *Final Fantasy 7*, exploring the slums of a futuristic fantasy metropolis of Midgar as Cloud, a fabulously-coiffed blond twink with an outrageously-sized sword and a cadre of scantily-clad lady warriors who cast protective spells on him. When Cloud gets too close to the edge of Midgar, a golden box with a line slashed diagonally across it appears in the center of the screen. "Warning!" it proclaims, and if I ignore it, the game will eventually turn Cloud around. This is a staple of even the most open of "open world" games: If you reach the edges of whatever digital world you're traversing, the programmers need a way to stop you. This is why so many games are set on islands or nestled into valleys with large surrounding mountains. To forcibly restrain a player who breaks the illusion.

When I wander my backyard, with its low wooden fence, its beans and corn, pansies and snapdragons, its discarded toys and telltale signs of toddler dominion, I am Cloud. We live on the edge of a mostly liberal neighborhood, which itself is on the very edge of a mostly liberal town, which is surrounded on all sides by deeply conservative countryside. We're living in a fantasy, our own Midgar, and I can feel the resistance when I get too close to the edge. But what I don't know is whether that resistance is our Midgar pulling me back in or the outside world pushing me away? Not just gay, really gay, with a gay husband. Gays with children! It's normal in our Midgar—but one step outside, and every force tells me to turn around.

When I look over my fence and into the forest, I feel a golden warning in my stomach, one that twists me back toward home if I go too far. Each step pulls me back, an electric tug from whoever or whatever programmed me and the world I traverse. But even though I have the illusion of freedom, I feel it shrinking.

Every once in a while, I get Cloud stuck somewhere that the

game's developers didn't mean for him to go. He twirls around and around, lodged in place, until I'm forced to hit the reset button.

Lately, I feel as if I've navigated myself into some unwanted space. I can see where I want to go. I can see my kids playing, my husband snoozing in the hammock, my dogs lazing in hot pools of sunlight. But I can't reach them. They can't hear me warn them. There is no spell I can cast to protect them. I have become a statue of polygons, stitched together by art and coding, spinning in a small, forgotten corner, with no chance of escape unless someone endeavors to reset me.

THE BEST FOR LUCY

Lea Waits

Lucy always froze on rainy days. Today was not a day to freeze. Mandy eased her through mobilizations so familiar they felt like a dance. She sprayed every creaking joint and squeezed a dollop of silicone into Lucy's left hip. Just in case.

Last month, the technician pronounced Lucy "perfectly average" for her age. "But let's keep an eye on that click. And her processors. With the proper care, Lucy might reach full potential."

"Of course," Mandy agreed. She only wanted the best for Lucy.

"Weekly socialization and a dab of Draxomil when it rains." The technician spoke as he scribbled on a blue pad. "You'll be amazed at her progress."

That blue scrap was tucked into Mandy's wallet as she huddled with Lucy beneath a charming portico that offered scant protection from the downpour. The portico belonged to Raquel Morris, a neighbor with a daughter around Lucy's age.

"Why, hello!" Raquel flung open the door and ushered them inside. "And *you* must be Lucy. Lucy, this is my daughter, Abby."

Sensing her cue, Lucy turned to Abby. "Hi. My name is … Lucy. What is … your name?" Lucy spoke slowly and extended her hand after a prolonged pause.

Abby took it smoothly. "Nice to meet you, Lucy. I'm Abby." Everything about Abby was smooth: her movements graceful and her voice finely-tuned to emulate human vocalization.

"Wow!" Mandy exclaimed. She'd never seen a KidBot as sophisticated as Abby.

"We are blessed." Raquel clasped her hands in the approximation of humility. "The 4K90s are technological miracles."

Mandy gasped, "4K? But they're not even—"

"On the market? Well, not for the general public. But if you have the right connections …" Raquel shrugged and winked conspiratorially. "I've been a Platinum Parent for years."

A Platinum Parent? Mandy had never met a Platinum Parent.

"How about Lucy, though? What a classic! I'm sure you've been pleased."

"Uh …" Mandy goggled. "Di–did you say you were a Platinum Parent? That's incredible!"

"You're sweet." Raquel demurred. "Well, we want only the best for our Abby. Platinums get access to exclusive enhancements and configurations not available to the average parent. It's not cheap, but the sacrifice is worth it."

Mandy wondered at the precise value of "not cheap" while Raquel peered into the playroom at the girls. "You should look into the program. You'll want the best for Lucy, and she's nearing end of life." Raquel leveled this judgment as casually as she had invited Mandy for the playdate. Now, she tilted her head, listening. "Does Lucy have a click?"

Stiffness was normal for a KidBot of Lucy's age. Clicks were not. To Mandy's horror, the first specialist floated the C-word. *Corrosion.* The second specialist agreed. He opened Lucy up, but found nothing but smooth, shiny metal.

"Defective coxa. Degenerative. Probably from the manufacturer. Too bad she's out of warranty."

They rode home in silence until Lucy asked, "Are you going to replace me?"

Mandy could swear she heard a tremor in the digitized voice.

To Raquel, Mandy said, "The technician thinks we have five,

maybe seven good years left. And then ..." She shrugged. "An overhaul."

"An overhaul?" A flash of naked horror crossed Raquel's features. Her brows knit in concern. "Surely, you'll want to up-grade to an affordable 460DL or a 3K. Platinum Parents trade up every three years, standard. Personally, I prefer every two. That way, the children are never outdated or underpowered. My Abby is barely scratched up. And she's never had a *click*."

Raquel's voice had dropped to a whisper, but Lucy's head rose an inch. Lucy's hip might be defective, but her audio processor was perfect.

Raquel continued, "Think of the surges, the crashes, the *corrosion*."

Mandy flinched at the word.

Raquel placed her hands on Mandy's shoulders. "Don't you want the best?"

"Of course," Mandy replied mechanically.

"If you want the best, let her go."

"But—"

"And then, *get* the best."

"You mean—?"

Raquel murmured in Mandy's ear, "It's easier if you name the new one Lucy."

"Mom?" Lucy's halting voice cut across the room. "Can ... we go ... home?"

At the house, Mandy dried the raindrops from Lucy's dull skin, which was pitted and grooved from a childhood of adventures. Then, joint-by-joint, she danced with her daughter until the rain lifted.

STEEL CAGE

Sally Toner

The average full-sized school bus, with passengers, weighs a little over 30,000 pounds. It has a no-crumple zone. It's meant to repel impact, not to absorb it. It will cut through anything it encounters on the road like tissue paper.

Tissue, thinner than skin.

When John is older, he will be applauded for his size. The bruhs will ooh and ahh at the gym, referring to him as an "absolute unit." He won't need steroids to bulk up. Just puberty, a couple of inches, some lifting before football season. They'll all cheer him on.

But today, he's in the seat behind the driver on the bus. His mother is the driver. She brought him to school to discuss what's going on with the other kids in class. The fifth-grade bruhs. John isn't a unit, yet. He's short, red-haired, freckled. He's about fifty pounds overweight with a milk allergy.

She's not sure how they ended up on Route 29. When her father, a unit himself, took her along on his tow-truck routes, showed her the ins and outs of large transport back in the day, there weren't cameras mounted on the ceiling. This one is high-tech, but these vehicles all follow the same rules of operation.

"Mom, where are we going?" John's voice is quiet.

He followed her after she beat the shit out of his teacher. She doesn't remember exactly how that happened. She went in to talk, just talk. But that asshole, with the dark brown corduroy pants and tan leather belt, hipster horn-rimmed glasses. Christ, she despises millennials. All needing a script. The dipshit teacher, caught off-guard, suggested they schedule a conference. The morning bell rang. She tried to explain her fears for John. He'd come home with bruises on his shins she suspected were from his tablemates kicking him, hard, from underneath. They could do that, turn his leg all shades of purple, yellow, green, like a field of bluebells and daisies. They could do it and not even scuff their goddamned white sneakers. So many white sneakers. Expensive brands. John had begged her to buy him some.

She honks the horn. Cars swerve. They're not used to a school-bus blast. She presses the lever to flip out the stop sign, turn on the lights so no one passes. Then it occurs to her that cars in the next lane might clip the sign. She pulls the lever back. Sees lights behind her.

She knocked the teacher's glasses off first. When he crossed his puny arms and took that tone, she landed a right hook. Her father taught her how to box, too. Number one rule, always get in the first punch. She just wanted to talk, anyway. Show the teacher the texts the girls sent John, pretending to like him, asking him to bring an extra ham sandwich, one of the special ones with vegan mayonnaise. They said they "thought gingers were cute." He showed the messages to his mother, so excited.

He didn't show her the other messages. When they sent him a gif of a laughing hog and typed: "Of course you like pigs. Boy piggies are UGLY." She only saw that when she snooped on his phone after he refused to eat for a week, scratched his arms until they bled.

The lights behind her are blue. And now sirens. The windows rattle, and the cab's metal shudders as she changes lanes. She and John are *Smokey and the Bandit*. He's never seen it. Maybe they'll watch it tonight.

"Mama, you're definitely going too fast."

He's still calm, but he never calls her Mama … just when he's had a nightmare, or he's really sick. Maybe when the other children screamed and huddled in the corner of the classroom while she kept throwing punches. One of them had red braces. This mama got red all over the teacher's corduroy pants. John may have also called her Mama when he ran after her into the parking lot. When they climbed aboard the bus with the keys still in the ignition. Driver on break. She knew what to do.

She sees lights ahead now. Flares. Waving. But they're in a steel cage. She knows that well. They'll cut right through, like tissue paper.

Thinner than skin.

LIGHT THERAPY

Jerica Taylor

In the first week of September, an event horizon jumps time-lines, and 46 children from my son's elementary see the stars close up and Earth far off. For .08 seconds, Leo floats weightless in the ancient sky.

They tell us our kids have been traumatized. A team of experts designs a tailored program for reacclimatization. The service is free. Two hours every day, my son sits in a chair and tells the provider that he did not go to space.

Because I don't have space shock, I am asked to leave the room.

Leo hides in his closet in the dark after, and only slides halfway out to share a peanut-butter sandwich with me. I lean against the door, and we trade bites.

After two weeks of daily visits from the provider, Leo does not hide in the closet anymore, so I think we're through the worst of it. But after a month of services, the provider says Leo isn't improving enough, and she needs to see him twice a day.

"We also have residential programs for severe cases," she offers encouragingly. "Most kids can at least say 'atmosphere' by now without having a catatonic revisitation. When he stares off at nothing, he's revisiting the space trauma."

I don't think that's what's happening.

One night at bedtime, I whisper to him what we've been warned never to ask: "Tell me about space. Tell me what you saw."

He comes alive in a way I haven't seen for months. Eyes bright, body in motion. He throws his arms out wide.

"You were an astronaut, weren't you? Did it feel amazing?"
His whole body pulses with the memory of joy.

The provider brings a lighter to the next session. She teaches my son how to use it. When I object, she abruptly picks up her things and heads for the door.

"He needs to learn to burn away the darkness one way or another," she says as she leaves.

I call the company and tell them we're discontinuing the service. They offer to match us with a new provider. They'll check back in a few days.

After school the next day, I find another lighter in Leo's backpack. "What are you supposed to do with this?" I ask him. I press the lighter into his face, ashamed even as I'm terrified. "Who gave this to you? Do you get the service in class?"

Leo takes the lighter and touches the flint to his tongue.

I snatch it away.

After a week of paranoia, I pull Leo out of school.

He dreams of going to space again. We talk about it, out in the backyard looking up at the stars. Neither of us speaks, but we both understand. He points to a spot just left of Orion. I think that's where he was.

In the dark, I wish on every atom of the universe that we could go there together.

WILD THING

Martha Lane

She conceived on her hands and knees, so it made sense to her that he came out with claws. Thick fur covered him in patches, the color of an oil slick. So black, it was almost green. She clung to him; he scratched her cheek. No nurse stepped forward to weigh him, to swaddle him, to welcome him. The monitor beep echoed, bouncing around cavernous mouths. He looked at her, blinked under too-bright strip lighting, from beneath a too-heavy brow. She cried out as she lifted them both from the bed and walked, blood still dripping, across the room to clean this child.

Gently, so not to hurt him.

By his first birthday, her forearms were an atlas of scars, glinting in the light as she gave him his present. A rattle. He crashed it onto the floor until it was dust. He left the wooden handle splintered, crawled away to eat ants. There weren't enough to satiate his hunger.

By his second birthday, her eyes carried bags that threatened to split as she gave him his present. A book. He barely looked at it, ripped it, created confetti from the thick board pages. He looked at her with hungry eyes. Panting. Approaching.

By his third birthday, her wounds had healed. She wanted to festoon the door with balloons like other mothers. Instead, a banner hung awkwardly from a dusty mantelpiece. A much-easier task with only two fingers remaining. Her hair now cropped short, short by necessity, was tucked behind her ears as she gave him his present. A small tin car. He turned it round in his hands, unsure. Tap tap tap, talons on metal. Tap, tap, tap, teeth on bone.

He howled until he was four.

By his fifth birthday, she no longer felt the incisions and tears. She no longer missed the feel of grass on bare feet or hot coffee on lips. She no longer heard the chewing at night. She flashed her knotted shoulder, giving him his present. Her final gift.

She held him. Gently, so not to hurt him. He beamed as he suckled and gnawed.

MOM TO YOU

Jennifer Murvin

My boy brought the mask home from a sleepover party at a friend's house. He wore it up to the door and I giggled at him, knowing he had worn it to make me laugh, to make a little joke for me. It pleased me to know he had thought to put the mask on for my benefit, that on the ride to my house, he had made a plan that involved me. At ten years old, more often I was of use to make food, do laundry, be an extension of the house or refrigerator, etc.

The mask itself was rubber, or whatever material creates that stinking, pleasing smell that takes one back to childhood, the excitement over a new toy, ball, pencil case. The particular chemical smell of cheapish distraction, not unholy.

It was not a Halloween mask, and if the mask were trying to represent a particular figure from history or entertainment, it had utterly failed, or I had missed that era or event or aspect of popular culture. The mask was simply a man's face. There was some semblance of facial hair, painted on, slightly raised. The eye holes were just large enough for a hit or miss; my son's eyes flickered in and out behind the holes. My son's shaggy hair fell just over the mask, so that I could not see the top, where it lay over his upper forehead. There was a sweet arc of freckles there, I knew, underneath the mask. I co-parented my son after the divorce; my son's father and I traded days, and this day, my son had arrived home from the three days away from me. I wanted to see his face. Sometimes, especially now in these preteen years, he would change so much, I would wonder who it was, exactly, walking to my door, that lanky body, those maturing features. What I'm saying is, I sometimes feared I would not know him, or that his father might return someone else in his place, hoping to fool me and keep our son for himself. I have this idea about my son's father because I had pondered the strategy myself, in the early days.

My son's voice sounded fuzzy inside the smelly, attractive plastic. "Do you know my name?"

I answered, "Why don't you introduce yourself? I can't invite a stranger into my house!"

He said, "My name is Jessup Miles."

This sounded to me like an old-timey cowboy actor. "Come on in, then, Jessup," I said.

He hugged me, so tall. He wore new shoes. This was not uncommon; my ex-husband was very wealthy, and my son would often come home with entire new outfits, shoes, haircut.

He resisted my requests to take off the mask. "Jessup Miles is home now!" he said, and his voice was his, my baby's. That hadn't changed yet, though some of his slightly older friends' voices were starting to deepen, to sound like their fathers'. He wanted macaroni and cheese, the microwave kind. "Thanks, Jen," my son said through the mask.

"That's Mom to you, bud," I said, with a laugh.

"Not to Jessup Miles!" he said. My boy, such an actor!

When he was smaller, it was *Star Wars* masks—Kylo Ren, Darth Vader. A period with Transformers. Spider-Man. Once, he had awakened me in the pre-dawn darkness wearing the Spider-Man, standing over my bed, and I screamed.

I searched "Jessup Miles" on the Internet, but nothing came up, and with the image search, no face resembling the mask.

The following morning, he came out of his room wearing it.

"Not to school!" I said, grateful to put the responsibility on someone else.

"It's dress-up day," my son said. He wore it and his new shoes, his hair tidily arranged over the mask. When he came home, he asked for pickles, which was not unusual.

That night, after he fell asleep, I tried to take off the mask, but it wouldn't budge. He raised his hand and pushed mine away; the eye holes were off, so I couldn't see if he did this with his eyes closed or open. I knew he was breathing, the mouth hole nice and large. I watched for a bit.

Jessup Miles requested oatmeal for breakfast, a single egg, poached. I looked up how to poach an egg on the Internet.

I called my son's father.

"It's a phase," he said. "Don't worry so much. I personally like it. It's funny. He's growing up. Accept that things are going to change."

I can't say I was surprised when my son's school pictures arrived home in the mail, and there was Jessup Miles. He was beginning to grow on me: the facial hair sweetly painted on, the rosy cheeks, the smile. I had not always gotten smiles before.

At least he won't have acne during his teen years, I thought. My son's eyes, when I could see them, danced underneath the mask. We met each other at the door, laughing. After his three days at his father's, he looked the same! I no longer worried if I would know him. What a silly bear I'd been, thinking his father would swap him! As if his father would be that smart to think of such an idea.

When I woke to my son standing over me in the pre-dawn, the mask smiling down, I laughed.

When his father took him on vacation and never came back, I filed a missing persons report on Jessup Miles. "His face, so distinctive!" I said. "That smell! Like a toy!"

Many, many years later, I came to the door after school as I always did on Wednesday, my usual day to take back the parenting. In the yard were so many of them! A garden of sons, Jessup Miles' comforting smiles, his five-o'clock shadows just right. I wondered which of them had the arc of freckles hidden there, under the plastic, but what did it matter? I invited my children inside.

ODETTE

Kelly Ann Jacobson

Alexie Fedorov, known behind the heavy red curtain as "Papa Rov," waits in the stage-left wing with one hand poised to push on the back of his newest dancer, Natasha. The orchestra has just finished tuning their instruments; the lights dim, and the crowd adjusts its own anticipatory pitch to a low murmur.

"I'm nervous, Papa."

Her back quakes slightly against his palm. The pattern of red and orange sequins there matches the leotard worn in the first performance of his late wife, Mila, even down to the color of the thread holding the seed beads in the center of the metallic disks. He should know—he was the one to sew it, back when they were so poor they had to rent a machine just to do the hems.

"Your fear is what makes you beautiful," Papa Rov whispers.

The curtain parts and shuffles back toward them. Natasha takes a deep breath. The music of the pas de deux begins, and Natasha's back stiffens as her brain system orders her muscles to their choreographed position. Alexie releases his hand as Natasha's working leg extends into a steady arabesque supported not, as the great Margot Fonteyn by Rudolf Nureyev, by a male partner, but rather by a moving pole attached to a harness around her waist that can extend her body up to five feet in the air. Now, it merely keeps her balanced as it slides her, en pointe in third arabesque, across the stage.

The pole is controlled by her brain system. Her brain system is controlled by Papa Rov.

The crowd erupts in applause for the beautiful dancer, originally christened D452 but now known by the press and its readers as Natasha Fedorov. She smiles, her face programmed to look down toward the floor and her mouth to slide up on only one side in a shy pleasure, and then the expression dawns as a bright and fixed focus.

Papa Rov has outdone himself with his new dancer, Natasha, one critic had proclaimed the week before. *She has all of the graceful beauty of national treasure Mila Fedorov, but the technical prowess we have come to expect from every member of the Rov Ballet. Every movement of her mouth, every flick of her fingers, reinforces the impression of human life.*

Mila would have burned the newspaper in the fireplace. Likely, she would have tried to burn Natasha along with it.

Your slaves, she called them when she did visit his laboratory. *You work so hard to make them realistic, and yet it is that attempt at human beauty that makes them so grotesque.* Yet, an aged dancer could not put bread on their table, so Papa Rov went out on the road with his traveling show again and again. By the time an investor took notice, Papa Rov was at work on D296—and Mila was dead. Now, he makes billions off the applications of his inventions. The dancers are just a passion project. He loves them.

And none more than his precious D452. In fact, Natasha holds such a special place in his heart that he has gifted her, on this day—her first birthday—a surprise. During her next lift, he has programmed her right hand to move behind her back to sign a series of letters—H-A-P-P-Y-B-I-R-T-H-D-A-Y-N-A-T-A-S-H-A—so that the motions are only visible to Papa Rov in the wing. The idea had come to him last night during dinner, and after she shut down for the night, he had made a few quick adjustments to her code to make her both enact the hidden message and become aware of it.

Here comes the lift.

Natasha's right hand descends. Papa Rov catches the micro movement of surprise on her face as her fingers flutter into H-A-P, and he begins to smile. Then something glitches. Her hand balls into a fist and squeezes. Her face still portrays joyful focus, her body perfect technical motion, and yet …

Papa Rov reaches for the control panel, but then Natasha's fingers move again into the letter H. His hand pauses in his pocket.

H-E-L-P.

The lift ends, and the crowd gives Natasha a round of enthusiastic applause.

THE WORRIED BABY

Meg Pokrass & Rosie Garland

Sherman's lips are rosy and full on the bottom. There is more than a grain of disobedience in his barely open eyes, born twelve hours ago.

"Woo woo, it's time to go!" a tall, lipsticked nurse says.

The pain drugs are wearing off, and they will not give me more. My legs are returning. "I'm calling him Sherman," I say.

"Like the tank!" she roars. She wants me to be happy, even without drugs.

"After my father," I reply, but she laughs right over me.

"I'm outta here!" yells Cheer-Up Nurse, and I feel a vibration in my neck.

I want to go with her, with anyone. To a movie, a bar, a crummy restaurant. Tired nurses complain like schoolgirls in the corridor.

"You got yourself a baby rebel, and you have to work your magic, Mommy," says another nurse, quieter but mean.

Sherman is not latching. Quiet-but-Mean Nurse glowers at me. I am so lucky, and it's unfair to be this lucky and so clueless. She looks at my baby as though she wants to take him and handle things right.

I think how a partner would be good at this moment. A husband to roll eyes with. Or a woman. Anything but the nothing surrounding my bed. Someone to say, "You two will soon be a milking team!"

My father did not live to meet his suckless grandson. I can hear the way he said on the phone *you were the funniest kid* when he called from the room he died in. I remember how his voice opened and closed with a squeak. People want a sepia child.

I sniff Sherman's worried hair, fiddle with his droopy little socks.

"What's wrong with my milk?" I query the doctor.

He winks, as if this is the most charming of maternal

questions. "Nothing is *wrong* with it," he says. "Your baby is too full of worries."

How can a baby be worried? What has he got to worry about? I didn't know then, how my breasts were killing machines.

There are mirrors we can handle together, and there are mirrors that are too much for us. By the time I have them removed, Sherman is married to a woman with glittery eyelids. She points her lips at my cheeks before planting them on my face.

"Mom," Sherman says. "We're worried."

"Sherman is not a worried old man," I say to my grown-up baby.

The face of my son has become like the moon, too dreamy to count on. If I could only drink a glass of milk without spitting it up, maybe his wrinkles would smooth out.

He does the cryptic. I do the quick. I gave him a head start, as he has to grapple with questions I can't make sense of. I used to hope we'd finish together, but he's always way ahead, or way behind. He hands me a warmed-up glass of milk and the pale light of worry pours from his face.

PHOTOGRAPH

Justin KB

My daughter likes to eat things. Bugs, buttons, woodchips, crayons, small toys—anything. I keep telling my wife, "God, I can't wait till she's older and grows outta this phase." I've been saying it for years now, but she hasn't grown out of it. Hasn't grown at all, in fact.

She should be nine, I think, or maybe sixteen. But she's more like four. There I'm standing, looking down at her somewhere amidst these interminable years of her childhood, and between the twin sickles of her (actual) shit-eating grin, there's a white corner blading out of her mouth.

"Give it," I say in something like an octave below my natural voice.

This commanding affect no longer has any effect. She runs around the corner into the kitchen, giggling. A little round head with a halo of wild hair peeps around the wall like a belated moon.

"Whatcha got?" I ask. My voice slips back into its regularly scheduled register, a tactical shift. Parenting is always this kind of war, prosecuted by idiots against an enemy that must win in the end, or else we all lose. I crouch behind her barrier and lie in wait. "Show me," I coo.

"Nunh."

"Please?"

She dares a peek in our no-man's land. I'm lain flat against the wall, clocking her movements by her shadow where it interrupts the sunlight streaming through the window.

"Where you gone?" she asks, leaning further into the abyss I've left for her. "Hello?" Her voice grows sharper as the void of the house yawns in her head. "Daddy!" she demands of the swelling walls.

I don't know why I don't answer her, but I don't. I shrink against the corner. In the shortening nadirs of her panic, I look down and see my hand has, in fact, been swallowed by the wall. Here, too, I can't tell you why I don't react. I can't tell you why I don't panic, or at least let her know not to panic. Let her know Daddy will fix this, it's fine. Instead I press deeper, growing smaller as her pleading declines into the resignation that I have, in fact, disappeared.

She's a puddle on the floor not two feet from me, consoling herself by gnawing on her fingers and screaming at the earth. The pile of her little body shakes with Pentecostal spirit at the injustice of loneliness. Silence follows wailing in an ebb and flow that builds toward crescendo, builds and builds, until it breaks on the abyss itself into nothing but an absence. When she stands, she's not little anymore. Not really. Not as she should be. Still too little, yes, certainly. Too, too little. The house will defeat her over and over and over at this size. But not so little as she was.

"Why did you let him go?" she screams, a little white corner still peeking from her lips.

"Why did you let him go," the walls answer.

At last, she pulls the thing from her mouth. It's small and square and solid white and blank. She holds it up, looking at it, its edges bloodied by its long, unnatural residence in sensitive flesh. Her breath hitches sharp as a hiccup. I press deeper into the wall because it hurts, and it hurts because I like it. I close my eyes and imagine the soft silent nothing of total wall-being, and I like it and it hurts to see anything else.

When I see her again, she's driving a nail into my forehead.

MONSTER SIGHTING, CIRCA MARCH 2020

Susan Calvillo

I arrive at the hospital for a "non-stress" test, which seems a silly name in these frightful times. The NST is administered in the same hospital where COVID-19 patients are admitted for treatment—same building, different floors. I hit a security checkpoint at the lobby's sliding glass doors, but someone's already in line. I wait outside to respect the six-foot-distance rule. A mother—who hopes her six-year-old has pneumonia because she dreads the alternative—cuts in front of me. I know she does not mean to. One person standing six feet back from another person doesn't look like a line. And this is an emergency entrance, and I don't look like I'm in an emergency, because I'm not—not yet.

I lose count of how many people in a bigger panic cut me. I'm invisible despite having three heads. None of the line-cutters wear masks, not even the sick ones. *Why am I* not wearing a mask? Or a helmet? Or an entire VAC suit? Finally, when there is a lull, a handsome nurse waves me forward. I imagine he has a five-o'clock shadow, or maybe three days' worth of five-o'clock shadows, which I can't see behind his mask. But he smiles with his eyes and gives me a medical mask, hand sanitizer, and a masked escort in scrubs.

The escort takes me to the next checkpoint. I undergo an interrogation in which all the correct answers are "no." My temperature is taken temporally. I'm given a new escort. I'm asked to sanitize my hands every time I enter or exit a space. Even though the escort presses the elevator buttons. Even though I touch nothing. The escort operates under the assumption that everything is toxic, including me.

I'm left in a lobby where the only two other people are wearing head-to-toe suits, masks, and goggles, an empty baby carrier between them. I try not to stare as I get flashbacks of all the science-fiction horror I've watched with my hands over my eyes. If this is a live-action film, where do I stand? Is the hero/virologist nearby in his lab? Are vomit zombies around the corner?

A technician finds me, straps me in for monitoring, confirms I have two heartbeats in addition to my own. And all three of my hearts are reacting at acceptable rates. Then before I know it, she puts me right back on an elevator, directs me to go *that way and just keep going and going.* This is the first time I have no escort, and I'm lost in a windowless corridor where every ten feet a sign says: STOP, GO BACK.

But the words are directed at medical personnel and staff, and the tone of that voice, *keep going and going,* drives me on. I take a long hall that turns and turns, then turns into rows of beds reserved for COVID-19 patients, lining the walls, a hundred or more. Empty, sterile, waiting.

A chill runs down my spine. I have stumbled upon a prophecy. These beds will be filled. Even in the dim light, the white bedsheets are blinding. I should not be here. I try not to breathe.

But the double doors await at the end of the hall. I see the first security checkpoint in their glass windows. The silence is eerie, but a sense of calm comes over me—I am safest when I am alone. The only germs in this sterile sanctuary are the ones I brought with me.

I put distance between the beds and me. I force my way out, bursting through the double doors. The staff on the other side jumps at the sight of me as if I'm a monster. Even the handsome nurse's hands go up in fright. And I realize my place in this thriller. I'm the jump scare. I am the monster. I have the potential to carry. But so do they. Eventually, we all will fulfill that potential.

BACK THEN, AT SEA

Kathryn Aldridge-Morris

I know what you're thinking. You're thinking: Who picks up her two-year-old son from preschool with beer on her breath, seaweed in her tousled hair, a borrowed T-shirt three sizes too big, and can't even walk straight, tripping on some baby in a car seat? Who doesn't recognize her own son waving from the play area, then sobs when he finds his own way into her arms? Who does that? And I'd probably be thinking that, too. But I don't have the command of your language, with your fancy Spanish subjunctive, your go-to tense for the unknown. And I am, it's true, quite drunk. My glasses are lying at the bottom of the Atlantic, and what started out as a fun day kayaking didn't end as planned: near drowning and sunstroke and rehydrating with two bottles of warm San Miguel because we knew we were late picking up, and if I said, "Mr. Magoo," to crack the ice that's formed over this baking hot Andalusian day, would you know who I meant? Maybe not.

Everyone thinks if you capsize in a narrow strip of water and you're an okay swimmer, you'll be fine. But I don't figure on unseen currents, on the wind whipping up, on anchored yachts that swing their full bulk at my head, speed measured in knots. And isn't that how I've been measured ever since I was pulled from the birthing pool, in knots, tied at regular intervals around an umbilical cord that cut off my son's oxygen? And what *about* my son, as I flail underwater on my first day out since he started kindergarten? What will happen to him, alone on the Costa de la Luz, if I don't make it?

When my son is four, I sit behind so many desks under spiraling ceiling fans waiting for answers. I'm able by now to pick out the subjunctive but stumble when one pediatrician says *idiopática*, fury spooling under my sunburned skin. My son's not an idiot for not speaking. That's how all-at-sea I was back then. We get no answers from audiology, speech therapy, child psychology. We just have a son who can't speak, is completely mute, and no one knows why. But I swear, when I'm seated in front of those experts in idiopathy, they get that same look in their eye, that look that asks: is that seaweed in your hair, beer on your breath?

Back in England, my son now six, I meet a neurologist, dapper in cream chinos, not a white coat. He smiles and draws me pictures of neurons wearing Stetsons—talks about cowboys trying to cross a river but how Red Indians are blocking them, and man, I want to say something, but he's the one with the crayon in his hand, and I need to see how the picture turns out and whether the cowboys make it, and I wish my son's recovery did not depend on genocidal metaphors. Medication might or might not take out the Red Indians. Then again, the cowboys—chin-deep in water, dragging their horses—could just need a little more time. He shrugs, seems pleased with his picture, at least.

When you need rescuing, you assume your rescuer will know what he's doing, have a basic understanding of wind direction, bring the right gear, not be stoned. But the kayak guy is paddling toward us without the one thing we need right now, and that's an engine. Does he think we're incapable, just can't be bothered? We're paddling, *mira!* He ties the kayaks together, sweep-strokes till we're turned around, thinking he can tow us across the estuary, but the current is working against us—now he gets it—and a fiberglass yacht caught by a wave rams us, flipping us three-sixty, dumping us into the water.

No one told us back then about rising tides and slowing currents, to hang on and wait for the moon to do its thing—how we just needed a little more time. When a boat with an engine does arrive, we no longer need it. Slumped, we paddle short, weary strokes. It must look so easy to those bathers unfurling towels for their babbling children on that perfect beach, cupping their hands over their seeing eyes, watching as we make it onto land, heaving the kayak up through the surf and onto the shore —our feet touching down on the hot, chattering shingle.

SOUL FUGUE

Olivia Campbell

T he trouble starts in childbirth, when your body gets sieved through the colander of motherhood, but your soul does not. As your baby erupts out the front of you, your soul squeezes out the back, hitting the wall and slamming unceremoniously to the ground. The baby is born, but the mother is not. You shake off the force of the blow from the cold, unforgiving hospital floor, then watch from afar as your body clutches the baby, as a nurse mops the blood from your body's trembling thighs, as your partner gingerly stretches down to kiss your body's forehead. Motherhood as an out-of-body experience, an alienation. Motherhood as a question mark rather than an exclamation point.

You watch as your partner pushes your wheelchair into the elevator but are so transfixed by the sight of your body holding a baby, you barely manage to slip through the closing doors behind them. You notice the dark circles cradling your eyes after two nights of little rest, nurses' pokes, baby's cries. You would have helped, but you weren't sure how. Your deflated belly ripples like punched-in bread dough, despite your body's painful insistence to get your uterus back to normal-sized. Have you always looked this sad, bewildered? Or is it just because your soul is missing?

The only thing that stops the constant cries is nursing. Always nursing. The sieving of your soul from your body has pulped your brain. Now it oozes out of your breasts. A child nourished by your body's undoing. Days blur into nights in a haze of cracked nipples, engorged breasts, spit-up, and diaper changes and never, ever enough sleep. The world crusts with a dull, grayish patina.

Your body wakes, feeling nothing. Nothing and rage. Nothing and resentment. Nothing and apathy, which is just feeling nothing about everything, isn't it?

You pace the tiny apartment—as much as a soul can "pace,"

anyway—while your body continues nursing, continues fading. The longer this separation goes on, the more difficult and unlikely reunification becomes. Down the street, an art museum (within walking distance!) beckons. Your body remains entombed on the second floor, burning boiled eggs and rarely mustering the energy for a shower. You want to scream at your body to get out there and live your life. To continue traveling and dancing and making friends and being curious. But nothing comes out. You are just a soul, after all, lacking a voice box. What does a scream into the void sound like when you're voiceless? How long can a soul survive without a body?

Even though he still won't accept any other caregivers, the baby has at least figured out day from night. "Show him the sun," the doctor said. *But I want to walk into the sun*, your body language seemed to say. You will your body to ask the doctor, "How do I get my soul back?" Should you get someone to sneak up and surprise you, like when you want to get rid of the hiccups? But physicians deal in the physical, not spiritual or metaphysical, and besides, your body isn't exactly aware of the true nature of the problem. At least not in any way that would've allowed for such precise articulation of language.

Is that you over there on the sofa? Your husk of a body carving a crevasse in the cushion deeper and deeper until eventually it swallows you up, cradling your body inside its contradictory recesses of soft fluffy fiber and cold metal springs. This is easier, your body decides. This is better for everyone. Will anyone even notice? A polyester tuft tickles your nose as your body becomes giddy, ecstatic even, pondering the prospect of finally getting some rest.

A scream erupts from the baby in his bouncy hammock, wresting your body from its dream. You hover closer to the open window. *Do I even want to go back?* you wonder as you watch your body flop out a heavy breast to stanch the screaming. But what is there for a soul to do without its body?

With a flash of sunset glinting off of the cars parked across the street, at last it dawns on you: all you have to do is make it through the day, so you can show him the sun tomorrow.

EFFERVESCENCE

Julianne DiNenna

O ur kids are ventriloquists, we parents the dummies that hang over their knees. Watch how we plunge to dirty floors on all fours when our babies drop their favorite spoons or figurines or beanies. Watch how we crawl under tables, stick our hands under couches amid dust and dander, grease or oil, to retrieve Minnie Mouse smiles or to soothe shrill screams till sanitized Minnie returns to sticky hands.

Watch us dangle from strings getting babies into bed, curtains drawn, lights low, and babies want suckers. "Dear Blessed of blessed mothers, safeguard our children, keep them safe from harm."

Fast-forward into the future, and their cries flash across our screens, not to ask how we are—not to ask if we would like a slice of the cake that they just posted on Instagram (the only medium we have left to actually see our kids and the friends they hang out with). No, no, I am not going to answer. No, not this time. I am going to enjoy my dinner. I am going to finish my soup, even if the phone sits next to my bowl.

No, they ask for cash, or how much soap goes into the laundry machine, how long it takes to cook a chicken leg. Or to accompany them to doctor appointments, sleep next to them during hospital stays, carry their bags, sit next to them during chemo sessions. No, Kahlil Gibran, our children really are our children. Their pain, our suffering. Their future, our fortune. The stunted arrows, our brokenness.

Here it comes again, another message, signaled by the ringtone set just for the kids, rhyme set to beat, and there we go again. Their house of tomorrow doesn't belong to us, but we pay their passage.

They're ours, and what are parents for, anyway, but to dangle on strings as near and as far away as possible.

THE IMPENETRABLE BOUNDARIES OF A TEMPORAL LOOP

Rachel O'Cleary

I don't know when I got stuck in the time loop. I'm afraid I may have been here for quite some time before I even noticed. I realize this seems like the kind of detail a person would spot straight away, but it's not exactly *Groundhog Day* in here. Or my ex-boyfriend's wedding day, or the day I die. It's just Wednesday. At least, I think it is. A gray Wednesday. The sky has been one long, low cloud for months.

On this day that I am stuck in, I am always awakened at the first sliver of dawn to the prickly sensation of someone staring. A large, brown eye centimeters from my face: Jamie, my three-year-old, needs the toilet.

On this day that has frozen around me, precisely three minutes into breakfast, someone spills a glass of milk on the kitchen table. Usually Jamie. Sometimes his sister, Sarah. Sometimes me. But always, always, the milk spreads everywhere. Dampens the bottoms of cereal boxes, drips between the leaves of the table and onto the floor. Dots the back of my neck as I crouch down to clean it up.

On this day that keeps me trapped, no matter what else I change, the following things happen: Sarah loses one shoe, Jamie needs the toilet the moment he is buckled into his car seat, we run out of yogurt and bananas, and I do exactly three loads of washing. I do this, even knowing the baskets will be full again in the morning, because the one and only time I didn't, my husband and I argued so bitterly that we might have divorced if I wasn't living in a temporal void.

I don't know why I'm stuck. In the movies, there is always something the main character needs to do to be released from the time loop, like win Andie MacDowell's heart or prevent a brutal murder. But as far as I can tell, my purpose here is to get from morning to night without allowing anyone I live with to be uncomfortable for too long. I have passed an eternity in the kitchen, vacantly sweeping up cracker crumbs while the clock ticks, the ceiling fan wobbles through its lazy rotation, and water swirls down the drain in a tight spiral.

I don't think there is a way out. I've been here so long that I'm beginning to forget things I once knew, like the capital of Colombia, the scientific name for the common blackbird, and what food tastes like when you're actually hungry.

I'm scrubbing the sink again when my phone rings.

"I just wanted to check in about tomorrow," comes my husband's voice.

"Tomorrow?" My chest bristles with gooseflesh.

"Tomorrow. Jamie's birthday. Do you need me to get anything on my way home?"

My knees wobble, and I drop into a chair. Remnants of spilled milk seep through my leggings, leaving a cold spot on my thigh. Cracker crumbs dig into my forearm where it rests on the table. It can't be Jamie's birthday. That's ages away. As it has been for months now.

The clock ticks, the ceiling fan wobbles through its lazy rotation, and water swirls down the drain in a tight spiral.

ENCLOSURE

Lindy Biller

I'm still sleeping when the school calls me. My son is sick, they say. I will need to come fetch him, and quickly. The zoo closes soon. The chaperones are not prepared for this, and I am his mother. I am the one who signed the permission form; there is no one else they can call.

By instinct, I check my phone. What time is it? Have I missed the ending? But the display is still pulsing: white numbers counting down on a black screen. Somehow, the numbers seem alive. I bring the phone back to my ear. The woman inside is adamant: My son has forgotten his lunch at home, has grown fangs and claws, and I should've expected this, naming him Lowell—the Old French for *little wolf,* a name I chose because it could mean anything, a first name or last, one syllable or two, a school or a street sign or a poet or a villain or the name of a song that always makes me cry.

"It means *little wolf,*" the woman says.

"I don't speak French," I say, but the woman hangs up, then texts me the address.

I am prepared for the worst. I am expecting blood. But I pass through the front gate and everything looks normal: the monkeys leaping from branches, the red pandas ambling up an angled platform, the otters twirling and flipping and somersaulting under manmade waterfalls. The zookeepers stare at me. I keep my head down, neck curved. I will know my son when I see him. I have brought his lunch, the one he forgot, and what am I supposed to do if not feed it to him? The yogurt will spoil. The milk will curdle. I was only asleep for an afternoon, a week at most, but his animal crackers are already stale, his buttered bread snowy with mold. There is a little folded note, grapes cut into quarters. No meat. For years, I've filed his claws and ground down his teeth and trained him how to hunger. Sometimes I make a game of it: We howl together, show the gleam of our incisors. I hold out an apple, and he eats it in three bites. A tray of brussels sprouts, and he sniffs at it, frowns, nibbles. A honey cake, which he devours. A rabbit, curled like a question mark in my hands, and we both wait, frozen.

The teacher comes out to meet me. She is all breathless and askew. "What took you so long?" she demands, elbows flapping like a crane's wings.

"I came straight here," I tell her, but she's not really listening.

She drags me along the path. I check my phone again. The countdown started on the day my son was born, and I don't know what it means. Maybe the numbers are a warning, or a cure. Maybe I'll understand them later. Maybe they'll slide softly into zero and life will continue, just as before.

"He's inside," my son's teacher says, pointing at the flamingo enclosure.

That was your first mistake, I want to tell her. Putting the flamingos indoors. I go to the fingerprinted glass and see them perched like lawn ornaments, flashes of pink in a shadowy black room. Slick black floors, dull black walls, a green hose snaking into a round tub. Windowless, unless you count the huge viewing window that all my son's classmates have crowded in front of. Their noses squish against the glass.

"Look," a child says—a human child, with hair and lips and skin.

I look. The flamingos are one giant pink umbrella with several thin, knobby legs for handles. Seven of them are drinking, heads scooped low. Five are preening, three or four just standing around. One is alert to my son's presence. Prancing, squawking. My son moves along the back wall, growls, and the others begin to notice him. Their heads turn, turn, turn, quick back and forths, like spinning ballerinas, or flamenco dancers—no, like sprinklers, the kind that spray short, frantic bursts in one direction, then jerk all the way back and start again. My son prowls toward them, and I see the white gleam of his teeth. The flamingos scatter, flare open and shut, as though clapping. The children gasp, fogging the window with their breath.

"Stop him," the teacher shouts.
But I cannot stop him. I watch, too, frozen.

THE BABY

Leah Claire Kaminski

The yard was full of clacking and buzzing and rustling, full of plants and insects and birds. Roaming her family's small property in the sub-rural zone of horse and palm farms, she stained her hands with palmetto berry and scratched her itches on thick-chunked bark of skinny slash pines, craning her neck up the trunks to the bright blue beyond. She liked it best when that blue turned black, or greenish-gray. Summer afternoon storms thrilled her to the bones, even better the hurricanes that glanced by once a year or so: air still, shadows erased, light lucid green. And then after, the steamy golden sweat of it.

She'd stay out past safety, till she felt her body adjust to new pressures, felt like a leaf blown and buffeted—felt identity-less. Which was the point.

Later she heard someone say they loved storms because it made their insides match their outsides, but it was more that her insides got pulled out, exposed, made incidental to the implacable wind, the unsparing rain, its fat drops thinning to wood-scouring needles.

One pre-storm morning she was busy in a nest of ferns, collecting plant parts. Rosary beads, lantana flower, papaya leaf, pinecone, air plant, coontie cone, fern frond, mahogany pod, bougainvillea bract. Ripping and knotting them, working to build a baby doll.

As she finished, a ladybug landed on the baby's flower eye. She shooed it off, held the baby's tiny mahogany arm. It was plump with strangeness and all hers. She could swear she felt it warming to her touch, sensed twitches from its vegetal thorax.

She started at her mother's voice screaming her in and looked up to a hulking wall of grayblack. The forest already stilled and strange. She ran inside. Baby dropped from her palm in her haste, its fern hand tearing away.

The storm was not what she loved, not this time—it was not

what she wanted. This was life made small by a world without thought, a world without want but to rip her apart. She'd dream about the howling wind for the rest of her life.

In the shocked after, she searched the strewn world for her baby's body, its squat coontie-cone trunk. She imagined it lifted by a driving arm of water and wind into the hurricane's eye, swirled up into the panoptic chaos, flayed and dismembered. Though she fretted, she never found it.

Navigating the spaces left between her parents' angles (angles sharpened by the sawing of powerless weeks and lost mementos and too-small insurance payments and too-crooked contractors), she learned to forget. Started college, moved north, met a guy. The rotted corners of her story falling away when she got pregnant. Thirty-seven weeks hit during a Midwest thunderstorm. A hurricane in the Gulf and a fire in the West, and here a tornado-bearing storm. She looked out the window as she labored and saw the wall of grayblack coming for them. Clouds festooning each other in ranks, shapes she'd never seen before, all dark, all dark, all piling on.

The storm dropped tornadoes like yo-yos and downed the trees and cut the power, and the baby came out perfect in the perfect middle of it. It turned its head to nurse; it slept on her chest all night. She stroked its downy head, her whole heart tumbling down into what she felt was the root of its life, its soft fontanel. It wasn't until early the next morning, in pre-dawn shadows, that she saw.

The baby's arm was wrapped in a papaya leaf. A banana spider resettled its legs over the soft belly button. She rubbed her eyes. Wished she could turn the lights on. Asked her boyfriend for water. Turned back. The baby's skin was bare, now. But she couldn't shake the resemblance. Her fitful nap-dreams full of storms, and of baby, the first baby. The one she'd lost.

The weeks went by. In the shadows, in the dusk and dawn, in the storms that still moved through, she saw that her baby's eyelashes were lantana florets, its fingers palm fronds, its tiny body a rough, pliable coontie cone. Her boyfriend didn't believe her. Her boyfriend left. She held her baby. She misted its body.

Knotted its mahogany-slice biceps tighter. She breathed in the wet blossomy scent of its little tummy. From its fontanel streamed the scent of rain on fertile earth.

ABOVE IT

Sierra Powers

Some kids are just bad sleepers. Every doctor, every article, every online mom group, echoed the same sentiment after listing every soothing method, every gadget, every feeding schedule that I had already tried. Full and clean and burped and bathed, my Ella never stopped wriggling and pawing and flapping and crying, no matter how tired she was …

Unless her window was open.

It faced the forest, thick and dark and full of hoots and howls and screeches. We played by the treeline only when the sun was still above it.

The first time I opened the window, the air conditioner had died and the fan was pure impotence, and I just needed to hear something besides her squeals. Which promptly ended when an owl's screech tore through the velvet darkness. Coyotes yipped a chorus that made her sky-blue eyes drift closed. Her chest rose and fell, clad in white cotton and bunnies. To do anything to disturb this dance was shameful to me. So I slipped away, stage left.

Six blessed hours later, I posted my success story online, to cast another line of hope to the sleepless. My head pain-free, my limbs feather-light, my eyes crystal-clear, I had found a way forward.

Until I was informed that I had exposed my child to threats of animal, bacterial, biological, and criminal nature. That I needed to record the sounds of nature and play them for her instead. That I needed to buy a portable air conditioner because money was nothing in comparison. That I needed to treasure every weary night because I could live to regret my shortcuts.

I did. I tried. To no avail, because when I was falling asleep with her in my arms, I would give in. And every morning, she would wake, bright-eyed, bushy-tailed, tangle-haired, and dirt-fingernailed. It wouldn't matter if the window was opened wide or just a crack. I'd have to bathe her before daycare, but the extra time was not a burden because I was equally energized.

I tried to stand my ground. I cited my sources. I tempered my tone and patiently, deliberately, explained myself over and over and over again. And when I caught myself taking pictures from her room of the forest to prove that civilization wouldn't dare threaten her, I stopped. I found a leaf in her crib with a strand of her tawny hair.

I deleted my account.

THANKSGIVING WITH THE CUELLOS: A TRIPTYCH

Alan Michael Parker

Holiday Bingo

Children, we're selling the pharmacy	The light amazes on her rhinestone glasses	WOW in the basement	The ghost smells like turpentine	Tammy brings José Cuervo Gold
The wind through the laundry, changing plans	Tammy, his secretary?	Pansies from her garden	"Ruben always gets the marsh-mallows"	Papi cuts his thumb
Sí soy americana	Garage drinking	**Mami**	Three desserts for Harry	It can't be a ghost
Mooney's ghost blows the kitchen fuse	Cowboys win!	The leaves so shimmery in reds and golds	Damn ants	"Chica, it's okay, we're not real cousins"
A ham from Dantwan the cop	Ruben & Esther do the cleaning up	If it's a ghost, it's a Mooney	"I'll drive Tammy home"	The loud ones are Pro-Choice Democrats

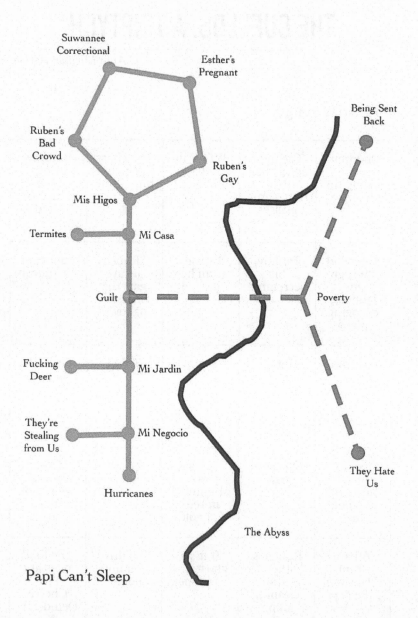

Papi Can't Sleep

Ruben and Esther in Their Old Room

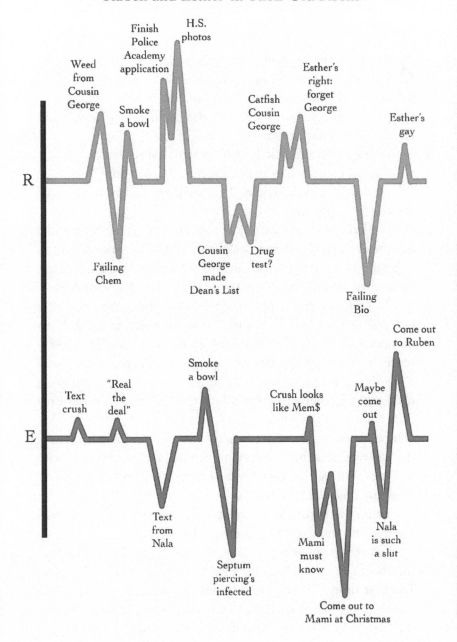

I AM THE TIDE

Jas Huff

B ehind your empty bed, behind the gathering dust, at the bottom of your stars-and-planets mural, I found a door. Or not a door, but the outline of one, painted over time and again, with no visible hinges. I pushed, and the outline gave way, and I crawled into a past, moments I thought lost.

I'd forgotten how the house felt with blank walls.

You sat on your bed, expecting me. "Hi, Mommy," you said.

I sat down next to you and gathered you in my arms—I am the tide, and you the sand.

I yelled at you in my study as you pinched my leg from under my ancient oak typewriter desk—inherited from your Meemaw —giggling because you thought we played. I yelled louder than I meant to, and my heart melted as tears welled in your eyes.

At first, my pain rippled out simply, pen to notepad after notepad. I filled my study with swells of paper, as if my heart pumped ink, before I began on the walls, in the middle of a sentence, as if a billowing tide brought my pen to the shore. Soon a sea of black ink engulfed all surfaces. I carved on the desk, used my fingernails to scratch into the old stain job, until my fingers bled on my paper. I used a pocket knife your father left behind, wrote all over the top of the desk, under the desk, inside the drawers, flushing them of my old life and filling them with my grief. Filling them with you. I moved out of my study and filled the house with you, too.

Your father painted moons, planets, and stars on your bedroom walls; you told me you visited them.

I wrote on those walls the past I saw when I went through the door. Your birth. Engulfing your miniscule body in my arms. The first time I let you sleep in our bed because you said eyes stared at you. The first time I let you cry yourself to sleep. The first time you told me, "You're my best friend, Mommy." Your life broke over me—salty and cold—never-ending waves of memories. I pushed through the door, the tide carrying me out.

A doctor told me you had a condition, genetic. I asked about the beach outing for your fifth birthday, "Will he be okay?" The doctor said you'd be fine, just fine. The medication swallowed all our worries. You played with a toy, pushed beads from one side to the other. The light gleamed off your wild curls, your hand on my arm as you stood and wrapped your arms around my neck. Scent filled my heart with warmth as you said, "I love you, Mommy."

Today—your fifth birthday—the sea folds like crumpled paper. Breakers crash against a rocky shore, froth spurts into the air. I recognize these rocks. You laugh, jump, stomp, gallop through the surf, hand engulfed by your father's.

No matter what I do, I end up here.

This is the last time joy crosses your face. This is your final giggle. This is when I realize: your eyes roll back, you fall into the swells.

Panic flows into every fiber of every muscle. My hands pull you up, but the sea crashes into us, pulling you back down. A flash in your eyes, a pained pleading as loud as a scream; I always saved you from pain before. Your hand pinches me trying to hold on. Blood streams from your nose, mixes with the white froth like red ink on paper. I can't save you.

I return to this moment, a tide to shore, never saving you, killing you over and over in the trying.

A PARENT'S WORST NIGHTMARE

Bryan Betancur

I woke to a tickling on my cheek. My eyes opened wide. Did I stir when a spider tried crawling into my mouth?

Arachnologists the world over agree: The odds this grotesque scenario would ever occur are nearly zero. Spiders have no interest in humans, nor their beds.

Soundbites from the documentary I watched before bed replayed in my semiconscious mind as I anxiously imagined a spider treading through my coarse stubble.

Our breaths and heartbeats emit vibrations that signal danger to spiders and discourage them from journeying across our sheets.

Sure, I thought unexpectedly, but what about *baby* spiders? Without my constant vigilance, my toddler engages in all manner of dangerous behavior. Just that afternoon, she picked up a dead squirrel in the playground and nearly swallowed a drill bit while I secured a bookcase to the wall. Keeping her safe is nonstop, exhausting work.

If your mouth is open in the middle of the night, you're likely snoring. Spiders would be wary to approach a dark hole reverberating disquieting sounds.

Bullshit! No amount of cautionary yelling would dissuade my daughter from ambling excitedly into a pitch-black cave.

An arachnid's survival instincts guarantee you'll never swallow one.

Tell that to a baby spider, condescending jerk!

Your body is similarly programmed to evade danger. You would instinctively rouse from the deepest slumber if bristly spider legs rubbed against your face.

That was precisely what happened! For all his supercilious declamations about arachnid survival behavior, the narrator failed to mention two equally potent forces: infant curiosity and paternal love. A baby spider *did* stray from her web and summit my bed. She was too minute to disturb my weary-dad sleep, and too insignificant to merit consideration from the evidently childless narrator. A larger arachnid, the baby's father, followed close behind, navigating that tenuous line between nurturing a healthy spirit of exploration in his daughter by granting space to roam, and quashing her inquisitive impulses by restricting her movement. Then the unthinkable happened—how easily it could happen to any of us! While watching his daughter from what seemed an appropriate distance, a burst of speed no one would expect from an infant propelled her into my mouth. He hurried after her, but the rapping of his weightier limbs against my skin snapped me awake. The earth beneath him quaked, and the entrance to the cave collapsed, trapping his baby inside. A parent's worst nightmare! The mortified dad scurried down my cheek and onto the nightstand, where he could safely determine how to save his daughter.

> Today I saw it up close. How it struggled
> to extend its countless legs
> in every direction.

The narrator's austere British accent was suddenly replaced by fragments of a César Vallejo poem I hadn't read in years.

> It's a spider that trembled, fixed
> to the edge of a stone;
> its abdomen on one side,
> and its head on the other.

The verses transported me beyond the limits of science and reason, to a place no aseptic nature documentary would venture. Vallejo's words evoked a visceral sensation that all living beings are slaves to the same ineffable forces of a ruthless universe. I couldn't allow the dad spider to suffer any longer. I rolled onto my side and turned on the baby monitor screen. There he was, standing deathly still on the corner of the nightstand. Despite the threat of my presence, the spider remained defiantly motionless.

> Seeing it today,
> paralyzed in its plight,
> I felt such sorrow for that wanderer.

The spider's agony for his lost baby stifled his flight reflex, overpowered whatever instincts the callous narrator posed as superior to a father's love. The longer I contemplated the un-flinching arachnid against the glowing image of my daughter resting peacefully in her crib, the more I felt the spider's fear, guilt, and desperation as if they were my own.

> *I thought about its eyes,*
> *about its countless legs …*
> *And I felt such sorrow for that wanderer!*

"We're in this together," I finally whispered, knowing he would find solace in the mystical bond that linked us in our shared experience of fatherhood. I shoved the rigid spider in my mouth, swallowed hard.

I took a long, loving look at my daughter, then switched off the monitor. As I drifted back to sleep, I wondered if I would ever tell her about the empathy she inspired in me that night.

The quoted poem lines in this story come from "The Spider" by César Vallejo, first published in 1918, public domain.

DIZZY LLAMAS

TJ Fuller

T ime loses the vertical hold. My seven-year-old, Lucy, will never know what that means—the way televisions used to skitter
and the little knob that grabbed control—but she can see the
house lost in time. The room has no idea what year it is. Fills
with Rogers from every year I've been stuck in this town. I choke
on a beer bong and fingerpaint the fireplace and steal my mother's menthols and try to protect my daughter.

Eight-year-old me won't stop lighting matches. Sixteen-
year-old me cannot carry a tune. I try to hide the Rogers, but
there are too many. Lucy glances between the old ones and me.
She asks about their comic books and golf clubs. The other Rogers are not as annoyed. They show her squirt guns and magic
tricks before they waver away.

I knew this house was glitchy. The living room used to fill
with forms of my mother, smoking and preaching and fighting.
She taught me to settle the time. Straighten it. And as I got older, I rolled it on purpose, so I could see her high again, so I could
see her cry at records, brush her hippie hair, giggle and chase
the neighbor boys.

I cannot focus long enough to regain the room's balance.
Lucy needs my attention. She has the attention of thirteen me's,
and it is not enough. She shows all of us her stuffed sloth and
handstand. How will Lucy explain what happens here? Time
opened too many tabs? Time had a media-playback error?

My mother called it the skips. "This is your fault," she said
to me. "You were supposed to be the missing piece, the stability
this house needed."

I had expected the same, a distance from the old Rogers,
something unfamiliar about their easy sweat and loud doubt.
Lucy lets one swing her around, but he vanishes, and she falls.
Shit. I shouldn't curse.

I grab her ten-year-old Roger's candy. "Hey," he calls and

disappears.

The hold is loose long enough that other versions of Lucy start to blip in and out. With her thick wail and darling wobble. With her fat, black eyes and penciled toes. Sleepless me arrives. He cannot burp his daughter because he is afraid of killing her. He stares into her mewl and feels her funeral. I know. I can still feel it. I wonder, if I let us keep slipping, if I would get to see preteen Lucy, smoking Lucy—her with a beer in her hand and a boy on her phone.

"Look!" I call to sleepless me and point to today's Lucy. "She makes it this far." But I am in the anchor moment. The Rogers rolling in and out don't remember where they've been. I am the one who has to hold on to this. To let it matter to the Rogers to come.

"Lucy," I call. "Let's play dizzy llamas."

We spin. She is free to blur, but I have to keep an eye out— that's the point of the game, me the first to the floor to break her fall. She revs up, and I wait for the reeling to be too much.

THE SHADOWS THAT REMAIN

Christina Tang-Bernas

Sonia ties the thin laces of her blue sneakers. The left one, then the right one, one bunny ear, two bunny ears, loop-de-loop, pull tight, there we go.

Outside, the sun is setting, the sky a purple and orange and dusty-powder blue. Her mother always nags at Sonia that it's dangerous for a woman to walk alone after dark. Why can't she get her exercise during the bright light of day, get some Vitamin D, you know, it's good for your skin, makes it glow, you know, you look so tired, Sonia, so tired, and, and …?

Sonia makes her way to the front door. Her feet weave deliberately around the scattering of colored wooden blocks and the stuffed cat toy that used to be white but is now an indeterminate gray, lying belly-up in the middle of the rug, careful not to disturb where they lie.

"I'm going out," Sonia calls over her shoulder, not expecting an answer as she steps out.

Rafael is in his office on the other side of the small house, as usual. Sometimes she's tempted to see if he's actually working like he says he is, but she never does.

A turn to the left, a few blocks, then a right, and she is on the main street of her neighborhood. The light from the streetlamps falls on her shoulder as she walks underneath, throwing her dark, distorted shadow out before her. A second shadow bobs beside it, a third of the height of her own shadow. The top is wavy, hinting at hair as curly as hers is straight, as curly as Rafael's hair. It disappears where the sidewalk is unlit and reappears at the next streetlamp, flickering in and out. Sonia does not look over at the empty space next to her, just watches the two shadows side by side.

In the half-darkness, she isn't as exposed, as scraped raw, no expectations of how she should express what it is she does or doesn't feel, how grief should or should not look. There is no guilt, no explanations, no awkward offerings of comfort or anticipations of reciprocity.

Just the soft sounds of footsteps, the low rumble of passing cars, and the two silent shadows flung before her.

She still gets the urge to put out her hand as she crosses the streets, waiting for a small, warm hand to slip into hers, but it never does. She tells herself it's not like a car is going to do any more damage.

Too soon she's back in front of her home. It's dark here, no streetlamps.

"I'm back," she calls out.

Rafael looks up. His weary eyes match hers. She sits on the sofa and leans against him.

She'd told him once about her shadow companion. And he'd confessed about the blurred, laughing reflections he would see on his computer monitor.

Rafael had once joined her on her walk, but the small shadow had not appeared. Maybe his much-larger one had blotted it out. Just like her reflection may have blocked out the ones on Rafael's monitor when she had sat beside him in his office, heart in her throat, waiting. Or maybe it was just because this was their "thing." Or maybe—

Rafael sighs. "How was your walk?"

Tomorrow it will be one year since. "Do—Do you think she's actually here?" she asks. The question sounds overloud in the stillness of the dim room.

"Do I think her spirit or soul is actually tied to us somehow, and she is actively trying to pass along some message?" he responds. "Or do I think this is just some leftover lingering echo of her life? Or do I think it's all in our minds, and we're clinging onto these 'things' so we can keep moving forward?"

Sonia shrugs.

Rafael is silent for so long that she peers over to check if he's somehow fallen asleep on her. "Does it really matter?" he finally says.

Sonia looks down at her blue sneakers.

—These shoes. *You have to get these ones. Blue is my favorite,*

Mommy—

She stands up, heading to their bedroom, but stops midway, staring down at the floor. Her hands clench at her sides, then unclench. Sonia bends down and picks up the stuffed cat from where it's lain since the day their lives shattered. It's softer than she remembers. She continues walking.

THE EMPTYING

Jessi Lewis

In the pale waiting room, I say, "My water broke, and I'm losing liquid," and the nurse says, "Maybe it did." They run a test. This is the rise, rain shifting to hail. Later, after the big push, my heart rocks while blood drains into the sheets—I release so much more than anyone lets on. I think, *I'm a mom,* and I think I hear the nurse say, *Maybe you are.*

In the week before, somewhere, I read that they were taking virus precautions and keeping fresh babies isolated with their mothers. But this is incorrect. After you come to the oxygen, you are buttery, still not yet real, even as I hold you. Forty people are circulating through the room. Their breaths could be pulsing with a virus that daintily falls into a pattern on your sleeping chest.

At some indistinct hour, one nurse simply rolls you away, down the hall, to extract a sample from your heel. Suddenly, you are a child, not just a thought, and I try to follow the lurching wheels. I'm livid, whipping my head around as though the corners of the corridor can direct me. My gown is stained with lochia.

I say, "I want her in the room."

A nurse says, "It's easier in the nursery."

I think, *I don't give a fuck what's easier.*

Her eyes say: *Your Depends is done for.*

I am certain that an orderly is smoking outside, my kid in the crook of her arm, a cigarette ashing over the swaddle, leaving burn spots in the muslin. So, I decide to search this hospital and drag my blood in a trail over false tile. I'm barely held together, though, spilling everywhere, and walking is shockingly difficult, in a way that nobody warned about. I am wounded, feral and captured, but not really, because I'm not thinking of escape.

I'm thinking of you.

And then I recognize that I don't know what I am. I might

just be loose blood in a beat-up bag.

Another nurse pads over to convince me that my baby is returning. I don't believe her softness or her health.

They do bring you back, eventually, rolled in, calm. I am leaking still, and I feel foolish, yet still livid. My insides steam as they empty. I'm certain that soon the doc will find my heartbeat dropping, my chest collapsing in on itself, bitterness pouring out in green sludge between my shoulder blades. All of me will just be a slurry on the tile floor.

I'll say, *I'm dying,* and the nurse will say, *Maybe you are.*

We have another night. The staff won't leave us to sleep, and I am growing sharper. I gnash my teeth at them.

Your eyelids are nearly transparent, and I curse at the emergency light. Clearly you have come from somewhere very dark, and that's the kind of environmental detail that I should be able to maintain. Every room is under a watery whiteness.

Suddenly, my body means less. My cotton mask goes missing. The nerves in my hands freeze until they are touching your forearm.

When I sleep four hours, the floor drowns slowly with red, two inches of me. A crimson swamp pools on the fourth floor. Somehow, it drains by morning. I watch, bleary. The walls are off-white again and the mattress is just pink.

That's when we break out. They want to see the car seat to be certain it exists, but instead, I leave with you on my lap in the wheelchair. My uterus leaks in the parking garage, along the highway, the exit, the narrow roads of the valley, and then our dirt driveway. I try to imagine this as a line of poppy petals following us, but really, it's just my iron mimicking the yellow centerlines. Over miles. I realize that I have made all of your cells, my cells, and all of the red I'm drawing across the map. I am vast. I am still livid.

"Do you know," I ask, "you're already making your own eggs?"

Meanwhile, your hands just clasp and unclasp as you consider each new ceiling and sky.

LANDFALL

Jiksun Cheung

In the time that my mother has been missing, the skies have turned a gray, roiling mass. The radio is calling it the most violent typhoon to make landfall in thirty-two years.

We've looked everywhere and there's nowhere else left except here, in the ruins of the abandoned Wah Fung housing estate, where my mother and I once lived in a tiny room on the sixth floor.

In the clearing outside, a squall tears at my flimsy raincoat and drags an old banyan tree snapping and splintering to the ground. A battered *No Trespassing* sign flits overhead and ricochets off the crumbling façade. I find an embroidered shoe near the entrance, swirling in the ankle-deep floodwater like a goldfish in the murk.

"Ma! Is that you in there?"

In response, there is only the whistling of the wind.

What on earth could she be doing here—and why now?

I try to recall the last time we were all together: Maggie, the boys, me, my mother, sitting around our dining table. The food getting cold. The nursing-home pamphlet opened to the page where an elderly couple beams at the camera, surrounded by family.

"If that is what you have decided," she says. And then, after a pause, she adds: "You always choose what is best for your family."

She doesn't smile. She doesn't pat my hand to reassure me that she understands. She doesn't touch the fish cheek I place in her bowl. But her words slide between my ribs so that even after Maggie and I clear the dishes and the boys are fast asleep, even after my mother quietly shuts the door to her room and turns off the light, all I can hear is: "You always choose what is best for you."

I stumble through the flooded corridors, flashlight in hand, until I see the old provisions store, tucked beneath the stairwell, where my mother used to work.

The shutters on one side have collapsed, revealing a row of empty shelves. I think of my mother stacking tins of oily fried dace, her thick, black hair in a knot, the radio behind the counter crackling a Teresa Teng love song. She pauses in front of the radio before changing the channel and then tells me to finish my homework before she locks up.

I find the other shoe on a landing about halfway up, water-logged and torn at the sole. The whistling continues unabated.

I step into my childhood home at the end of a long corridor on the sixth floor. The room is empty, save for the candle on the floor painting the peeling walls a flickering orange, and the figure by the window struggling with the handle.

"Ma—are you hurt?" I say. "What are you doing?"

She is surprised to see me, but then her expression hardens. "It's rusted shut," she says. "Can't get it open."

"Come on, Ma." I put an arm around her shoulder, but she pulls away.

"Just let me do this," she says.

"Come on—we shouldn't even be here."

I take her by the wrist, but even now I'm surprised by her strength. She wrenches free and bangs a bony fist onto the rusty handle. A cry of frustration escapes her lips.

"Ma—have you lost your mind?" I shine the flashlight on her hand where an ugly purple blotch is already pooling beneath the skin. "We can talk at home."

"I didn't ask you to come."

This is what happens when we talk: words fly out of our mouths, but we never seem to understand each other. "What do you want, then, Ma?"

"Just—help me," she says. "Please."

Outside, the rain surges like waves on rock. The whistling is louder, too, coming from all directions, rising and falling, as if seeking harmony but never quite finding it. I realize she'll never leave this place until she does whatever she's here to do.

"Fine," I say.

I raise the heavy flashlight and bring it down sharply on the handle. Once, twice. A crack, and then something gives way. The window explodes, ejected by a mighty pressure. The candle goes out. And I remember.

The day of the big typhoon, thirty-two years ago.

Ma says the store will be flooded, so I wait for her under the dinner table, wrapped in a thick blanket. The wind whistling all around. Suddenly, the window bursts open, and I'm engulfed by a sound that I can feel in the pit of my stomach, a deep thunderous drone: beautiful, like the long, solitary call of a blue whale, but also infinitely terrifying, like the howl of some unfathomable beast, so loud that even the floor shakes.

I curl up into a ball under the blanket and call for her, not realizing that she is already beside me.

"I'm here," she says, pulling me deep into her arms. "It's all right. I'm here."

My mother listens now, silvery-white hair plastered to her face, enraptured by the haunting harmony of the typhoon barreling as it did a lifetime ago, along winding corridors, between cracks in the walls, and through the room on the sixth floor with the open window.

She finds my hand and clutches it, now and in the past. We listen for a while.

"I'm here, too," I say.

"I know."

LESSONS I WILL TEACH MY SON

Kendra Fortmeyer

To care for cast irons: after cleaning, immediately dry and wipe down with a towel dipped in oil, until they glisten.

When you think fondly of someone, tell them.

Don't listen to people who say *should, should, should.*

Each new experience, even unpleasant, is intrinsically interesting. Pay attention.

Fairytales endure because there is something true in them. (See also: myths, legends, mountains.)

In fairytales, there's a magic and a danger in the number *three.*

Sunsets are slippery things—enjoy them swiftly.

For sauces: let onions cook fully before adding tomatoes or wine.

For hurricanes: Stay away from the windows. Hunker on the good, dry wood of the floor, next to me.

If you are thrown into water so deep that you cannot tell which way is up, carefully let a single bubble of air slip from your lips and follow it to the surface.

Never walk away from a pot of boiling oatmeal.

Never forget: your feelings are valid.

Never listen to people who say *shh, shh, shh.* If someone is trying to drown out your voice, ask yourself why.

Ocean waves break (*shh, shh, shh* on the shore) in sets of three.

Sea-level rise will happen in your lifetime. I am sorry for this. I didn't do it, but I was there.

If someone tells you to keep something secret from me, *especially* if they are hurting you, tell me immediately. *No matter what.* Tattoo this in your bones.

The high tides are highest when the moon is full, but also when it is new. Which is to say: question what you think you know.

For example: do not heed the singing of the sea-cliffs at night.

And: if a green-eyed girl with hair cascading like sunset-kissed waves bids you follow her to the beach (the waves coming in *shh, shh, shh* on the shore), don't.

(Really. Don't.)

Beware, too, the talk of dull-eyed men with the scent of sea-weed on their breath; their minds are barnacle-hollow, and their masters would have you share their fate.

Beware *especially* the singing of the sea-cliffs at night.

If you are ever doused in drink and fool enough to walk the sea-cliffs at night, and meet a girl with green eyes and hair cascading like waves beneath the full moon, and she extends her hand, do not take it.

Do not become doused in drink.

After an ice storm: nick tree bark with a thumbnail to see which limbs survived. Look for a pale moon of green.

(But do not trust reflected moons. Do not trust sea green.)

Do not trust promises written in sand.

Do not trust whispers that *you are our chosen one*.

Do not accept invitations down dark alleys. Even if they're doused in promises that they know something about you. Know why you've always felt different. Do not trust whispers that you will rule beneath the waves.

Do not listen, especially, to whispered lies about your mother by green-eyed girls or the distant singing of the sea-cliffs. Insist they have me mistaken for someone else.

Move through the world with the lightness and freedom that comes of being nobody special. Feel the lightness of the wind in your hair.

Remember that to be nobody special is a blessing. That to be a prince is to be a target for assassination. That kings never die peacefully of old age.

Remember to appreciate the small things: The warmth of the sun on your skin. The singing of the crickets in the tall, fragrant grasses. The juice of a fresh peach, running down your chin.

Remember, on your weakest nights, when the full moon pulls shining at the tides, to stop your ears with wax against the singing of the sea-cliffs. To write down the small pleasures (sunshine, grasses, air) in groups of three, to read them fiercely, over and over, like a spell that can keep you here.

Make yourself strong, because I cannot always protect you. Write your own spells, because mine cannot always keep you here.

… and if none of these things: if you find yourself, doused or no in drink, sinking beneath the waves with the hands of green-eyed girls twined in your hair and the singing of the sea-cliffs in your bones, remember how I love you, how before you breathed I loved you. And forgive me for all I've done: how I took you from everything, to give you the sun.

AUTHOR *biographies*

REBECCA ACKERMANN is a writer, artist, and designer in San Francisco. Her work has appeared or is forthcoming in *The New York Times*, *Wigleaf*, and *Barren Magazine*, among other publications. For more of her writing, find Rebecca at rebeccaackermann.com and on Twitter at @rebackermann.

BARLOW ADAMS is a writer and the father of three children who are better looking than they have any right to be considering they share his genetics.

KATHRYN ALDRIDGE-MORRIS is a mother of two, living in Bristol, who writes flash fiction and creative nonfiction. She was recently shortlisted for the Bath Flash Fiction Award, and her work appears in *Ellipsis Zine*, *Lunate*, *Janus Literary*, *The Phare*, *Reflex Fiction*, *Brilliant Flash Fiction Anthology: Vol 2*, and elsewhere.

MADELINE ANTHES is the Assistant Editor of *Lost Balloon*. You can find her on Twitter at @maddieanthes, and you can find more of her work at madelineanthes.com.

JUSTIN KB is a writer in the Atlanta area. His work has appeared in *Rattle Magazine*, *Barren Magazine*, *Dovecote*, and elsewhere.

AMY CIPOLLA BARNES has words at *FlashBack Fiction*, *JMWW Journal*, *Popshot Quarterly*, *X-Ray Lit*, *Janus Literary*, *Perhappened*, and elsewhere. She's a *Fractured Lit* associate editor and *Gone Lawn* coeditor. Her debut collection, *Mother Figures*, was published by ELJ Editions. A full-length collection is forthcoming from Word West in 2022.

DeMISTY D. BELLINGER is a mother of tween twins, a writing professor, and a writer who lives in Massachusetts. She nursed her girls for nearly two years.

BRYAN BETANCUR is a Spanish professor and freelance journalist who writes about Latino identity and representation. His creative work has been published in *iōLit*, *The Nasiona*, *The Rush*, and *Hispanic Culture Review*. He lives in New Jersey with his wife and daughter.

LINDY BILLER grew up in Metro Detroit and now lives in Wisconsin with her family. Her fiction has recently appeared or is forthcoming at *Pithead Chapel*, *Flash Frog*, *X-Ray Lit*, and *Chestnut Review*.

MELISSA BOWERS is the winner of the 2021 *SmokeLong Quarterly* Grand Micro Contest, the *F(r)iction* flash fiction competition, the *Breakwater Review* Fiction Prize, and *The Writer Magazine*'s inaugural personal essay contest, and her work was selected for the 2021 *Wigleaf* Top 50. Read more at melissabowers.com.

EMMA BREWER is a writer from Vermont. Her work has been featured in *McSweeney's*, *The New Yorker*, *Hobart*, *Fractured Lit*, *Jellyfish Review*, and elsewhere.

AUDREY BURGES writes in Richmond, Virginia. Her debut novel, *The Minuscule Mansion of Myra Malone*, is forthcoming in January 2023 from Berkley/Penguin Random House, and her work also appears or is forthcoming in *McSweeney's*, *Pithead Chapel*, *Hobart*, *Cease, Cows*, and other outlets. More of her writing is available at audreyburges.com.

SUSAN CALVILLO is a Chinese/Mexican-American mother of 2020 twins and the author of *Excerpts from My Grocery List* (Beard of Bees). Her writing can be found in *Nightmare Magazine*, *Eye to the Telescope*, *Zyzzyva*, and *New American Writing*. Keep reading at susancalvillo.com. Follow on TikTok at @thatbeardlessbard or on Instagram at @susan_calvillo.

OLIVIA CAMPBELL's work has appeared in *The Atlantic*, *The Cut*, *History*, *The Guardian*, *The Washington Post*, *Smithsonian Magazine*, and *Literary Hub*. Her first book, *Women in White Coats: How the First Women Doctors Changed the World of Medicine*, was published in March 2021 by HarperCollins/Park Row Books.

TARA CAMPBELL is a writer, teacher, Kimbilio Fellow, and fiction co-editor at *Barrelhouse*. She received her MFA from American University. Previous publication credits include *SmokeLong Quarterly*, *Masters Review*, *Wigleaf*, *Jellyfish Review*, *Booth*, *Strange Horizons*, and *Craft Literary*. Her fifth book, *Cabinet of Wrath: A Doll Collection*, dropped in June 2021.

JIKSUN CHEUNG is a short-fiction writer from Hong Kong. His work is published in *Wigleaf*, *SmokeLong Quarterly*, *The Molotov Cocktail*, and elsewhere. He and his wife share their home with two boisterous toddlers and enough Play-Doh to last a lifetime. Find him at jiksun.com and on Twitter at @JiksunCheung.

KELLE SCHILLACI CLARKE is a Seattle-based writer whose stories have appeared or are forthcoming in *The Penn Review*, *Los Angeles Review*, *Leon Literary Review*, *Gone Lawn*, and other journals. She was recently awarded the 2022 Pen Parentis Fellowship and is on Twitter at @kelle224.

CHRISTOPHER DeWAN is the author of *Hoopty Time Machines: Fairytales for Grownups*, a collection of domestic fabulism from Atticus Books. He has published more than fifty stories, is featured in *Best Small Fictions*, and has been nominated twice for a Pushcart. More at christopherdewan.com.

JULIANNE DiNENNA's poetry, essays, and short stories have appeared in *Rattle*, *The Journal of Compressed Creative Arts*, *Rise Up Review*, *Months to Years*, *Adanna Literary Journal*, *Unruly Catholic Feminists*, Stanford Medical blog, *Gyroscope Review*, *Italy, a Love Story*, and *Offshoots*, among other outlets. Her poetry collection, *Girl in Tulips*, is forthcoming.

JAMIE ETHERIDGE's work has been published in *JMWW Journal*, *X-Ray Lit*, *(mac)ro(mic)*, *Bending Genres*, *FFF*, *Coffin Bell*, and *Inkwell Journal*, among other outlets. She placed second in the 2021 Versification Contest for Mosh Pit CNF. She tweets at @LeScribbler.

MELANIE FIGG is the author of the award-winning poetry collection *Trace*. Her poems and essays are published widely. She's won many awards for her work, including a National Endowment for the Arts Fellowship. As a certified professional coach, she offers workshops and writing retreats and works remotely with writers. Find her at melaniefigg.net.

ERIN FITZGERALD is the author of *Valletta78*. Her stories have appeared in *Hobart*, *Barrelhouse*, *Wigleaf*, *Salt Hill*, and elsewhere. She lives in Connecticut, and on Twitter at @gnomeloaf.

JENNIFER FLISS (she/her) is a Seattle-based writer whose writing has appeared in *F(r)iction*, *The Rumpus*, and elsewhere, including the 2019 *Best Short Fiction* anthology. Her flash collection, *The Predatory Animal Ball*, is out from Okay Donkey. She can be found on Twitter at @writesforlife or via her website, jenniferflisscreative.com.

KENDRA FORTMEYER is the author of the novel *Hole in the Middle*. Her short fiction has been awarded the Pushcart Prize and featured in *Best American Nonrequired Reading*, *One Story*, *LeVar Burton Reads*, *Lightspeed*, and elsewhere. She is a graduate of the Clarion Science Fiction and Fantasy Writers' Workshop.

TJ FULLER writes and teaches in Portland, Oregon. His writing has appeared in *Hobart*, *Vol. 1 Brooklyn*, *Juked*, and elsewhere.

ROSIE GARLAND writes long and short fiction and poetry and sings with post-punk band The March Violets. Her latest collection, *What Girls Do in the Dark*, was shortlisted for the Polari Prize 2021. Val McDermid has named her one of the most compelling LGBTQ+ writers in the UK today. Find her at rosiegarland.com.

CAROLJEAN GAVIN's work is forthcoming in *Best Small Fictions 2021* and has appeared in places such as *Milk Candy Review, Barrelhouse,* and *Pithead Chapel*. She's the editor of *What I Thought Of Ain't Funny*, an anthology of short fiction based on the jokes of Mitch Hedberg, published by Malarkey Books.

MIRIAM GERSHOW is the author of *The Local News*. Her stories have appeared in *The Georgia Review, Gulf Coast,* and *Black Warrior Review*, among other journals. She lives in Eugene, Oregon, with her husband and son, where she is perpetually at work on her next novel.

DIANE GOTTLIEB writes fiction and nonfiction—all of it true. Her work has appeared in *About Place, The VIDA Review, Hippocampus, The Rumpus, Brevity*'s Nonfiction Blog, and *Entropy*, among other outlets. She's the prose /creative nonfiction editor of *Emerge Literary Journal*. You can find her at dianegottlieb.com and at @DianeGotAuthor.

AUBREY HIRSCH is the author of *Why We Never Talk about Sugar*, a short-story collection, and *This Will Be His Legacy*, a flash-fiction chapbook. Her stories, essays, and comics have appeared in *American Short Fiction, The New York Times, Black Warrior Review, Time,* and elsewhere.

JAS HUFF (she/they) employs IT witchcraft for money while studying word sorcery for an MA at University of North Texas. During her free time, she practices gender morphing and parent demonology.

KELLY ANN JACOBSON is the author of many published books, including *An Inventory of Abandoned Things* and *Tink and Wendy*. Kelly earned her PhD in Creative Writing from Florida State University and now teaches fiction.

MEAGAN JOHANSON writes from her lair in Oregon. She has been published in *Fractured Literary, Janus Literary, Emerge Literary Journal,* and elsewhere. She loves music, books, new obsessions, and anything with butter on it. You can find her on Twitter at @MeaganJohanson.

LEAH CLAIRE KAMINSKI is the author of three poetry chapbooks. Find more recent work in *Boston Review, Massachusetts Review, Prairie Schooner, The Rumpus,* and *Zyzzyva*, among other outlets.

LYDIA KIM is a writer based in the Bay Area. Her essays and fiction have appeared in *Catapult, Ursa Minor, Had,* and *Longleaf Review*. She's an alum of the 2021 Tin House Summer Workshop in fiction.

STEPHANIE KING has won the *Quarterly West* Novella Prize and the *Lilith* Short Fiction Prize, with stories also appearing in *CutBank*, *Hobart*, and *Matchbook*. She received her MFA from Bennington and serves on the board of the Philadelphia Writers' Conference. You can find her on Twitter at @stephstephking and online at stephanieking.net.

MASHA KISEL holds a PhD in Slavic Languages and Literatures and currently teaches at the University of Dayton. Her writing has been published in *Gulf Coast*, *Columbia Journal*, *Vestal Review*, and *Prime Number Magazine*.

NAZ KNUDSEN is an Iranian-American writer and filmmaker. She holds an MFA in Writing–Creative Nonfiction from Lindenwood University. She has a translated screenplay and several essays in Farsi. She lives with her family in Durham, North Carolina.

LEONARD KRESS has published fiction and poetry in *Missouri Review*, *Iowa Review*, and *Harvard Review*. His recent collections are *Walk Like Bo Diddley* and *Living in the Candy Store and Other Poems*, and his translation of the Polish Romantic epic *Pan Tadeusz* by Adam Mickiewicz was published in 2018. Find him at leonardkress.com.

MARTHA LANE is a writer by the sea. Her flash has been published by *Sledgehammer*, *Perhappened*, *Bandit*, *Reflex Fiction*, and *Ellipsis*, among other outlets. Balancing too many projects at once is her natural state.

JO SALESKA LANGE lives and writes in St. Louis, Missouri. She received her MA in literature with an emphasis in rhetoric and composition from the University of Missouri-Columbia and works as an academic writing coach. She is currently pursuing an MFA in fiction from the University of Missouri, St. Louis.

JESSI LEWIS grew up on a blueberry farm in Virginia. She was *Oxford American*'s Debut Fiction winner, 2018. Her work has been in places like *Zone 3*, *The Hopkins Review*, *Pinch*, and *Yemassee*. Jessi was a finalist for the PEN/Bellwether Prize and mentioned in *Best American Short Stories 2020*.

JAMI NAKAMURA LIN is the author of the illustrated speculative memoir *The Night Parade* (Custom House/HarperCollins, 2023). An NEA US-Japan fellowship winner and *Catapult* columnist, she has been published in the *The New York Times*, *Catapult*, *Electric Lit*, and many other publications.

MEAGAN LUCAS is the author of the award-winning novel *Songbirds and Stray Dogs* (Main Street Rag, 2019). Meagan's short work has been published in journals like *Still: The Journal*, *Monkeybicycle*, and others. She is the editor of *Reckon Review*. She lives in Western North Carolina with her husband and children.

JL LYCETTE is a mom of three humans and a physician who discovered her inner writer on her journey back from burnout. She writes speculative and medical fiction, and was a 2019 Pitch Wars mentee. Her creative nonfiction was awarded third place in the Willamette Writers 2021 Kay Snow awards.

MIKE McCLELLAND, like Sharon Stone and the zipper, is originally from Meadville, Pennsylvania. He has lived on five different continents but now resides in Georgia with his husband, their two sons, and a menagerie of rescue dogs. Find him at magicmikewrites.com.

MAUREEN McELY is a writer of short fiction and screenplays. She has written for *McSweeney's* and was a Nicholl Fellowship semifinalist in 2021. She lives in Cincinnati, Ohio, where she splits her time between writing, caring for her small children, and navigating life with a neuromuscular disease called myasthenia gravis.

DW McKINNEY is an associate editor at *Shenandoah Literary* and a senior editor for *Raising Mothers Literary Magazine*. She lives and writes in Las Vegas, Nevada. Say hello at dwmckinney.com.

FRANKIE McMILLAN writes poetry and short-short fiction. She lives in Aotearoa New Zealand. Recent work appears in *Best Microfictions 2021* and *Best Small Fictions 2021*. Her short-short fiction book, *The Wandering Nature of Us Girls* (New Zealand Canterbury University Press) is due out in August 2022.

K. C. MEAD-BREWER lives in Baltimore, Maryland. She is a graduate of Tin House's 2018 Winter Workshop for Short Fiction and of the 2018 Clarion Science Fiction and Fantasy Writers' Workshop. For more information, visit kcmeadbrewer.com and follow her at @meadwriter.

EDIE MEADE is a writer, artist, and mother of four in Huntington, West Virginia. She is passionate about literacy and collects books like they're going out of style. Say hi on Twitter at @ediemeade or at ediemeade.com.

KERI MODRALL RINNE is a 42-year-old mother of two. She graduated from San Francisco State's journalism program and freelanced extensively before shifting into the fulfilling work of writing for environmental and community organizations. She has remained quietly committed to stories and poetry and recently completed her first novel.

VERONICA MONTES is the author of the award-winning chapbook *The Conquered Sits at the Bus Stop, Waiting* (Black Lawrence Press, 2020) and *Benedicta Takes Wing & Other Stories* (Philippine American Literary House, 2018). Her work has been published in *Wigleaf, SmokeLong Quarterly, Cheap Pop, Fractured Lit*, and elsewhere.

JENNIFER MURVIN's essays, stories, and graphic narrative have appeared in *Diagram, The Sun, Indiana Review, American Short Fiction, Cincinnati Review, CutBank, Phoebe, Southampton Review*, and other journals. Jen is an assistant professor at Missouri State University and the owner of the independent bookstore Pagination Bookshop. More at jennifermurvin.com.

RACHEL O'CLEARY studied creative writing at University of Wisconsin-Milwaukee. She currently lives in Ireland with her husband and three children, writing mostly very short fiction in between school runs. You can read her work at *Reflex Fiction, Ellipsis Zine, Strands Lit Sphere, Janus Literary*, and other outlets. She occasionally tweets at @RachelOCleary1.

ALAN MICHAEL PARKER is the author or editor of eighteen books of fiction, poetry, and scholarship. He holds the Houchens Chair in English at Davidson College. He served as a judge for the 2021 National Book Award in fiction; it was a lot of reading.

MANDIRA PATTNAIK's writing features in *Best Small Fictions 2021, Citron Review, Passages North, Dash, Miracle Monocle, Timber Journal, Bending Genres, Watershed Review, Amsterdam Quarterly*, and *Prime Number Magazine*, among other outlets. Pushcart, Best of the Net, and Best Microfictions nominated, her fiction has been translated and received Honorable Mention in the *Craft* Flash Contest 2021.

MEG POKRASS is the author of nine fiction collections, and her work has appeared in hundreds of publications, including three Norton Anthologies of the flash fiction form. She is the founding editor of *Best Microfiction*. Meg lives in Inverness, Scotland.

SIERRA POWERS balances child-rearing, fiction writing, and cookie-baking with the grace of a Weeble Wobble. No, she cannot fix your computer without bribery, especially since she is a UX designer by day now. She lives in Wichita, Kansas, with her child, spouse, and dogs.

PIP ROBERTSON lives in Aotearoa New Zealand with her partner, daughter, and dog. She has stories published in *The Reading Room, Landfall, Hue and Cry*, and *Jellyfish Review*.

MELISSA SAGGERER has flash in *Barren, Tiny Molecules, Milk Candy Review*, and elsewhere. Follow her on Twitter at @MelissaSaggerer.

CAROL SCHEINA is a deaf speculative-fiction author who also works as a technical editor in the Washington, D.C., suburbs. Her short stories have appeared in *Escape Pod, Daily Science Fiction, The Arcanist*, and other publications. You can find more of her work at carolscheina.wordpress.com.

LAURA STANFILL is the neurodivergent author of *Singing Lessons for the Stylish Canary*, forthcoming from Lanternfish Press in April 2022. She's the publisher of Forest Avenue Press, and she wishes on indie bookstores like stars.

JAN STINCHCOMB is the author of *The Kelping* (Unnerving), *The Blood Trail* (Red Bird Chapbooks) and *Find the Girl* (Main Street Rag). Her stories have recently appeared in *SmokeLong Quarterly, Atticus Review*, and *Ligeia Magazine*. She is featured in *Best Microfiction 2020* and *The Best Small Fictions 2018* and *2021*.

CHRISTINA TANG-BERNAS, when not out exploring the world, lives in Southern California with her husband, her human-daughter, and her cat-daughter. Her work has appeared in *Sci-Fi Romance Quarterly, Strange Constellations*, and *Twist in Time*. Find out more at christinatangbernas.com.

JERICA TAYLOR is a nonbinary neurodivergent queer cook, birder, and chicken herder. Their work has appeared in *Postscript, Schuylkill Valley Journal*, and *Feral Poetry*, and their prose chapbook of linked flash pieces, *Donuts in Space*, is available from Gasher Press. They live with their wife and young daughter in Western Massachusetts.

JOANNA THEISS worked as a public defender, government attorney, and health researcher before becoming a freelance author. Her publication credits include articles in academic journals and popular magazines, and her short fiction has been published in literary journals such as *Barren Magazine* and *Inkwell Journal*.

MICHAELLA THORNTON is a fan of second acts, sweet and spicy tea, and soul music. She hopes to do for thunderstorms what Mary Ruefle did for snow. You can find Kella procrastinating and dreaming on Twitter at @kellathornton.

SALLY TONER is a high-school English teacher who has lived in the Washington, D.C., area for over 25 years. Her poetry, fiction, and nonfiction have appeared in *Northern Virginia Magazine, Gargoyle Magazine, Watershed Review*, and other publications. She lives in Reston, Virginia, with her husband and two daughters.

LESLIE WALKER TRAHAN's stories have been featured in *The Forge, New Delta Review, Gone Lawn,* and *SmokeLong Quarterly,* among other publications. Her story "Good Teeth" won the 2020 Ryan R. Gibbs Award for Flash Fiction. She lives in Austin, Texas. You can find her at lesliewtrahan.com.

ERIC SCOT TRYON is a writer from San Francisco. His work has appeared or is forthcoming in *Glimmer Train, Willow Springs, Los Angeles Review, Pithead Chapel, Monkeybicycle, Fractured Lit, X-Ray Lit, Longleaf Review,* and elsewhere. Eric is also the founding editor of *Flash Frog.* Find more information at ericscottryon.com.

ADDIE TSAI (any) is a queer nonbinary artist. The author of *Dear Twin,* Addie holds an MFA from Warren Wilson College and a PhD from Texas Woman's University. *Unwieldy Creatures,* their queer biracial *Frankenstein* retelling, is forthcoming from Jaded Ibis Press. They are editor-in-chief at *just femme & dandy*.

LEA WAITS writes speculative fiction and is fascinated by heroes-next-door, the social life of machines, and moral dilemmas involving wormholes. Her work has been featured in *The First Line* and recognized for Silver Honorable Mention by the 2021 Writers of the Future Contest. Follow her on Twitter at @leawaits.

K. S. WALKER writes dark speculative fiction. Their favorite stories include monsters, magic, or love gone awry. When not obsessing over a current WIP or their TBR list, they're outside with their family. You can find them on Instagram at @kswalker_writes.

DIDI WOOD's stories appear in *Wigleaf, SmokeLong Quarterly, Jellyfish Review,* and elsewhere. "Rattle & Rue," originally published in *Cotton Xenomorph,* was chosen for the *Wigleaf* Top 50 in 2019. Find her at didiwood.com.

MARIANNE WORTHINGTON is cofounder and poetry editor of *Still: The Journal,* an online literary magazine. Her work has appeared in *Oxford American, Calyx, Chapter 16,* and *Cheap Pop,* among other places. She grew up in Knoxville, Tennessee and lives, writes, and teaches in southeast Kentucky. Say hello on Twitter at @m_worthington.

ABOUT THE *editor*

HANNAH GRIECO is a writer and editor in Washington, D.C. She has written for *The Washington Post, Al Jazeera, Parents Magazine, Today's Parent,* and *Huffington Post,* as well as for a variety of anthologies and literary journals. Find her online at hgrieco.com.

ACKNOWLEDGMENTS

- "Bad Boys" was previously published in *Jellyfish Review*.
- "Fever Dream" was previously published in *Fifth Wednesday Journal*.
- "Mom to You" was previously published in *Fiction Southeast*.

"Soul Fugue" Author's Note: *"Soul Fugue" is dedicated to Julia Fine, because it was unearthed in the author's psyche by reading* The Upstairs House.

COLOPHON

The edition you are holding is the First Edition of this publication.

The bold title font is DIN, created by Albert-Jan Pool. The cursive font is Abuget, created by Khurasan. The Alternating Current Press logo is Portmanteau, created by JLH Fonts. The sanserif font on the back cover is Avenir Book, created by Adrian Frutiger. All other text is Iowan Old Style, created by John Downer. All fonts are used with permission; all rights reserved.

The cover was designed by Leah Angstman, with art elements by Comfreak and Nika Akin. The interior vintage artwork was digitized as follows: demon by Enrique Meseguer, hanging bat by Darkmoon Art, mouth by Clker, birdcage girl by Prawny, talon by StarGlade Vintage, angel by Gordon Johnson. The bird divider was created by Ocal, courtesy of Clker. The Alternating Current lightbulb logo was created by Leah Angstman, ©2013, 2022 Alternating Current. The photo of Hannah Grieco was taken by ©Gretchen Edwards. Images used with permission; all rights reserved.

All other material was created, designed, modified, or edited by Leah Angstman and Hannah Grieco. All material is used with permission; all rights reserved.

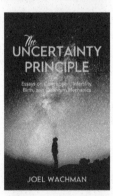
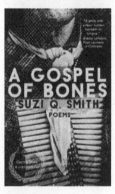

alternatingcurrentarts.com